#10

friends, cooking, eating, talking, life.

W9-CPE-092

Grosset & Dunlap

#10
A Measure of Thanks

friends, cooking, eating, talking, life.

By Diane Muldrow
Illustrated by Barbara Pollak

Grosset & Dunlap
New York

For John, Gretchen, and Wally Klindworth, with love—D.M.

Special thanks to Sondra Balouris Brubaker, and Mom

Thanks to Miriam Ruff and everyone at America's Second Harvest.
You can find out more about America's Second Harvest
at www.secondharvest.org.

Text copyright © 2003 by Diane Muldrow. Illustrations copyright © 2003 by Barbara Pollak.
All rights reserved. Published by Grosset & Dunlap, a division of Penguin Young Readers Group,
345 Hudson Street, New York, NY, 10014. GROSSET & DUNLAP is a trademark
of Penguin Group (USA) Inc. Published simultaneously in Canada. Printed in the U.S.A.

Library of Congress Cataloging-in-Publication Data is available.

ISBN 0-448-43201-3   A B C D E F G H I J

"Ooooh!"

"Wow. You really painted these yourself?"

"Shawn, these are awesome!"

Shawn Jordan's dark eyes lit up behind her cool lime-green cat's-eye glasses. "Thanks, you guys!" She set a pair of pale yellow teacups and saucers safely on a counter away from where she and her friends were cooking. The cups were accented with bright green flowery shapes. "I did these at this new place in Park Terrace where they sell you plain white dishes, and paints, and stencils if you want them. And you just sit at a table and paint! Then you leave your stuff there while they fire it in a kiln, and a week later you go back and pick it up. It's so fun!"

"Where are you gonna put them?" asked Amanda Moore.

Shawn looked around the Moores' large, bright kitchen. Cupboards with glass doors showed off the colorful dishes that Mrs. Moore collected. "I'm giving these to your mom," said Shawn, "'cause she likes funky stuff like this. Next time I go there, I'll paint her a matching teapot."

"She'll love them!" exclaimed Molly Moore, Amanda's twin. "They'll look fantastic in here with all her other cool things. I wish *I* could paint like you."

"Me, too," agreed Amanda.

"Mine would look like a four-year-old did it," said Peichi Cheng, giggling.

"So would mine," agreed Natasha Ross with a smile.

"Oh, anyone can do this," said Shawn brightly. "Next time, I'll take you all with me. Maybe I'll have my thirteenth birthday party there in April!"

"That would be different," said Natasha as she began to stir her homemade brownie batter.

Peichi slapped her forehead. "Oh, I just remembered! Guess *what*, you guys! Something funny happened to me on the way home from school today, after the twins dropped me off. I was almost home, and there was this squirrel running down the sidewalk toward me. He was really cute! Anyway, he kept running, like, right at me, and I thought, 'Hey, this squirrel isn't moving off to the side like squirrels usually do,' you know? And then it looked like it was gonna run right up my leg! It was *so weird!*"

"No way!" exclaimed Molly.

"Yeah! I thought it was gonna *bite* me! And, you know, I was carrying my big backpack, 'cause I brought all my books home this weekend to make book covers for them. Anyway, I started to back up as fast as I could but the squirrel kept coming! And pretty soon I was running backward down the sidewalk—really awkwardly 'cause I was carrying all those books!"

The Chef Girls shrieked with laughter.

"Then what?" cried Amanda.

"Well, I was also afraid that the squirrel—who looked like a baby—was gonna dart into the road, so I was, like, torn between wanting to get away from it in case it had rabies, and wanting to make sure it wouldn't get run over! So I screamed, 'Help, a crazy squirrel is chasing me!'"

Everyone cracked up at they pictured Peichi running screaming from a squirrel—backwards!

"So what happened?" asked Shawn, her brown eyes wide.

"Luckily, this man and this lady were walking by and they figured out what was going on! The man said, 'That looks like a *tame* squirrel! We'll get a box from the pet store down the street, and we'll capture it and take it to someone who knows how to care for orphan squirrels.'"

"No way," groaned the twins at the same time, which made everyone laugh even harder.

"...So then I just went home!" finished Peichi with a shrug. "That was nice of them, you know? To just take charge like that? I hope I remembered to say, 'thank you!'"

The Chef Girls shook their heads as they looked at one another and giggled. Peichi was always good for a laugh. None of her friends had ever really seen her in a bad mood—or when she wasn't expressing her cheerful personality with fun, colorful clothes and awesome, artistic hairstyles.

"Hooray! It's Friday!" Peichi went on. "Natasha, we're still having pizza at your house after we drop off this food, right?"

Natasha's pale blue eyes sparkled. "Absolutely," she replied. "We have to celebrate surviving our first week of seventh grade!"

"And finishing another successful cooking job!" added Amanda.

"You know, I can't believe that Dish is more than a year old!" exclaimed Molly. The Chef Girls, as they called themselves, earned spending money by cooking for people in their Brooklyn, New York, neighborhood of Park Terrace. Like the girls' own parents, these people were sometimes too busy with their jobs and families to make dinner every night, and were happy to pay for some home-cooked meals to be delivered.

Sometimes the Chef Girls cooked for no charge, just to help someone. They'd done this for new families who'd moved into the neighborhood, and for families in crisis. In fact, that's how Dish began. The twins' mom suggested that the girls cook a week's worth of meals to help out the family of their new classmate (and Amanda's crush) Justin McElroy, whose kitchen had been damaged by an electrical fire. Luckily, no one had been hurt, but the McElroys, who'd just moved from Chicago, had to move into an apartment while their kitchen was completely renovated. With Mrs. Moore's help, Molly, Amanda, Peichi, and Shawn made a ton of food—and the McElroys were touched that people who barely knew them had been so thoughtful.

Dish had changed since then. The girls had brought in Natasha, who they hadn't gotten along with in the past. But now Natasha was a good friend—and they knew she always would be.

It wasn't always easy for the girls to balance Dish with school, music lessons, and after-school activities, but the girls always had a great time cooking together. It could be a real adventure—they'd catered parties, cooked for huge families, and had recently been interviewed on a live morning TV show! The girls would never forget doing a cooking demonstration on national TV.

"*Ohmigosh!*" cried Amanda suddenly, looking up at the clock. "The chicken! Who's watching it?"

"I thought you were," said Molly.

"But—it's five-thirty! The timer was supposed to go off at five-oh-five! Why didn't it go off?" She quickly put on oven mitts and yanked open the oven door. "Oh-h-h," she groaned, as she carefully pulled out the chicken and set it on a heatproof trivet.

The girls gathered around to inspect the chicken. Amanda cut off a small piece where it wouldn't be noticeable, and looked worriedly at her friends.

"Dry?" asked Shawn anxiously.

"Yeah, it's dry. I ruined it! But why didn't the timer go off—" Just then, Amanda realized something. With all the talking and laughing, she'd been distracted...

"Uh, you forgot to set the timer, didn't you?" Molly asked her.

Amanda nodded miserably and looked down at the floor.

"Don't worry, Manda," Molly said soothingly. "It'll be okay. At least we didn't burn it."

"No, it *won't* be okay!" insisted Amanda. "We have to deliver this food soon! And it's too late to roast another chicken, even if we had one."

No one said anything, and Peichi nervously cleared her throat to fill the silence.

"*Mrow*," wailed Kitty suddenly. Even the Moores' fat tiger cat seemed to know something was wrong. Despite the problem, everyone giggled at Kitty, who was sitting straight up in a chair and watching the girls intently.

"Maybe we could turn it into something else," said Molly, "so that the Browns won't notice it's dry!"

"How are we going to do that?" asked Peichi.

"We'll make, like, a casserole or something. Or— a chicken potpie! We'll cut all the chicken up, and the creamy sauce that goes in the potpie will cover up how dry the chicken is."

"But we've never made a potpie before!" cried Amanda.

"Oh, I wish Mom was home from work. She'd know what to do."

Natasha pointed to Mrs. Moore's baker's rack. "Your mom has a ton of cookbooks. Or we could find a recipe on the Internet! There must be hundreds of chicken potpie recipes out there."

"But what about the ingredients?" Shawn pointed out. "We might not have everything we'd need, and—"

"And we don't have time to make the crust," wailed Amanda. "This is all my fault. I'm so sorry, guys. What are we gonna do? We don't have enough food for the Browns!"

"Let's check out the Internet before we freak," said Molly firmly. She led the Chef Girls toward the den. Somehow, seeing Molly take charge helped Amanda calm down.

Soon the girls had found a list of chicken potpie recipes on the Internet.

"Easy Chicken Potpie," read Shawn over Molly's shoulder. She chuckled. "That oughta do it! Click on it, Molly."

Everyone was quiet as the girls quickly read the recipe.

"Look!" exclaimed Molly. "This says to use biscuits for the crust. We don't have time to make biscuits from scratch, but, Manda, don't we have one of those 'pop-up' cans of biscuit dough? Mom usually keeps stuff like that around."

"I'll check," said Amanda, heading toward the kitchen. "What else?"

"Cream of chicken soup," called Molly over her shoulder. "And frozen vegetables. I know we have that. Luckily, Mom keeps the freezer full! Dried herbs..." she muttered, her green eyes scanning the screen. "We've got the rest of this stuff. Cool! Everything's gonna be fine—and we don't have to deliver the food for another hour or so."

Making the chicken potpie turned out to be easy. The girls threw out the chicken skin and bones, cut up the chicken, and put it in Mrs. Moore's 9 x 12-inch glass baking dish with a mixture made from cream of chicken soup, cream of celery soup, milk, frozen peas, and frozen corn. Then the girls lightly cooked some chopped baby carrots and added them, too.

"I hope this turns out okay," fretted Amanda as she sprinkled the mixture with celery seed and paprika. Natasha added some dried parsley.

"I think it looks delicious," commented Molly. "What's not to like? Everything in here is normal stuff."

"Well, it just makes me nervous to give a customer something we've never made before."

"You know, my mom said once that a 'real' cook is able to make a meal with whatever is around," Natasha told her friends. "So, Molly, you're a 'real' cook!"

Molly smiled. "Thanks!" She topped the mixture with the unbaked biscuits that had been cut in half. "You know,

8

I don't think we should bake this. When Mr. Brown's ready to eat it, he can put it in the oven. We'll put a note in with the food to tell him what to do."

"I hope he doesn't mind not getting a roast chicken," said Shawn. "Did we tell Mrs. Brown exactly what we were going to bring?"

"Well, I think I just said 'chicken,'" said Amanda. "So, this is chicken!"

"Chicken and biscuits, that's even better!" Molly pointed out, absentmindedly wiping her hands on her baseball jersey top. "It'll be okay!"

"It definitely will!" said Peichi, her long black ponytail swinging as she nodded. "When Mrs. Brown called to hire us, she was joking that Mr. Brown will eat anything—and that when she goes out of town to see her mother, she always worries he's gonna eat something that went bad in the fridge."

"Eeeeewwww!" cried the girls.

Half an hour later, the girls had packed up the food in plastic containers and carefully placed them in sturdy shopping bags. Taped to each bag was their cool business card, in case the client wanted to tell a friend about Dish.

The Browns' house was only two blocks away. One of the great things about living in Brooklyn was that the girls were allowed to walk around Park Terrace without their parents, as long as they were with a group of kids. And Park Terrace seemed to have *everything!* Awesome pizza...townhouses with stoops where people sat on warm evenings and talked to neighbors...dozens of restaurants that served food from all over the world...Prospect Park, with its huge lake and peddle boats, a skating rink, and a bandshell where people went to see free concerts and eat picnics in the summertime...and a subway which traveled under the East River into Manhattan—the Big Apple—New York City.

Molly rang the bell of the brick townhouse, and Mr. Brown, holding a chubby toddler, opened the door. "Hi, girls!" he said. "You're just in time. We were getting hungry, weren't we, Jason?"

"Hungry!" repeated the little boy, happily stretching out his arms to Peichi.

"He likes you!" said Mr. Brown.

"Hi, Mr. Brown," said all the girls as they filed in. They quickly introduced themselves and brought everything into the kitchen.

 "This is three-bean salad," Molly told Mr. Brown, removing the plastic lid so he could see inside. "You can keep all these containers. We include them in what we charge you."

"And this is a lasagna, still frozen," said Peichi. Sometimes on a Sunday, the Chef Girls made food ahead of time for future jobs, and stored it in the Moores' big basement freezer.

"Brownies!" said Natasha, patting another container.

"Here's, um, a chicken potpie," muttered Amanda. *Or, should I say a mystery potpie,* she thought to herself.

"Chicken potpie!" exclaimed Mr. Brown, flashing Amanda a big smile. "Wow! I *love* chicken potpie. I hope it's just like my mom used to make!"

The twins glanced at one another.

Yipes, Amanda told Molly with her eyes.

Molly and Amanda were doing "the twin thing," when they had the same thought at the same time.

Just like Mom used to make? That's a tall order! Molly's eyes flashed back worriedly.

Mr. Brown pulled out his wallet as he looked around at the girls. "Er, do I pay you individually, or—" He hesitated.

"I'm the treasurer," Peichi replied. "You can pay me! Then I'll pay everyone else."

"Are you sure?" Mr. Brown teased her, handing her a big bill. "Keep the change," he added. "Girls, thanks a lot. Everything looks just great!"

"Mine!" agreed Jason, pointing at the brownies.

Mr. Brown showed the girls to the door. "Thanks again. Come on, Jason, let's go have some of that yummy chicken potpie with those little pearl onions in it!"

After Mr. Brown closed the door, Amanda said with a nervous laugh, "Uh-oh—*our* chicken potpie doesn't have pearl onions in it!"

"Too late now! Come on, let's get out of here before he notices!" whispered Molly mischievously, and the Chef Girls took off running up the hill to Natasha's house, giggling like they'd just gotten away with something.

"Hi, Mom," called Natasha when she opened her front door fifteen minutes later. She led her friends into the stately foyer of her beautiful home. As they followed Natasha, the girls glanced at themselves in the massive mirror that hung near the door, over a beautiful antique table.

"Oh, hello, girls," said Mrs. Ross, gliding down the thickly carpeted stairs as the girls trooped inside. Her rose-scented perfume filled the hallway, and her steely blue eyes warmed for a moment as she brushed Natasha's blond bangs out of her eyes. "Hi, sweetheart. How did the job go?"

"Good!" replied Natasha. "We're going to order our pizza now. I'll see if Elizabeth wants to come down." Elizabeth Derring, who was in seventh grade with the Chef Girls, lived with her aunt on the top floor of the Rosses' house. The Derrings had moved to Brooklyn from Minnesota a few months ago.

"She's baby-sitting, remember?" Mrs. Ross reminded Natasha. "Well, it's a warm night—perfect for eating outside in the garden! I've set out some plates and glasses for you."

"Oh, okay. Where's Willy?" asked Natasha, looking around for her cute little terrier.

"He's out for a walk with Daddy. Sweetheart, you got a letter today—from Paris! I put it in your room."

"Yay! A letter from Laure!" exclaimed Natasha. Laure was a teenage friend Natasha had met in France, where she and Mrs. Ross had spent most of the summer. "I'll read it later. Right now I have to call Pizza Roma. I'm starving!"

After Natasha ordered the pizzas—one plain, one with pepperoni and mushrooms—the girls followed her outside to the garden.

"Is this your mom's china?" gasped Molly when she saw the Rosses' picnic table. "We're going to have pizza on your best *dishes?*"

Natasha blushed when her eyes fell upon the stack of large china plates decorated with an old-fashioned rose design. Pale-pink cloth napkins lay neatly folded near the beautiful china, along with monogrammed silverware, tall ice-tea glasses, and a pretty ice bucket.

"Believe it or not, these aren't our best dishes," she replied. "But I don't know why my mom thinks we'd want them for *pizza.*" She looked around at her friends and rolled her eyes. "You know my mom. Everything has to be really formal!"

"That's okay," Amanda told her. "She's just trying to make everything nice for you."

"That's how she shows you that she cares!" added Peichi, nodding enthusiastically.

"I guess so." Natasha tucked her blond hair behind her ears. "It's just that she always makes me feel so—different."

But even as she said that, Natasha wanted to take it back. Her friends were right! Looking at the beautiful table, she imagined her mom carefully placing all the pretty things on it, just so...Mrs. Ross hadn't always been the most affectionate mother in the past, and she could be really controlling and, well, stiff. But since their trip to Paris over the summer, Natasha and her mom had grown much closer. Natasha could tell that her mother was trying hard to make up for the past.

Thank you, Mom, Natasha thought gratefully. *Sorry. I love you, too.*

"Well, *I* think it looks nice," declared Shawn, interrupting Natasha's thoughts. She smiled warmly. "Our pizza will taste better on these plates than on soggy paper plates!" She tuned in the radio on Natasha's purple plastic boom box. "Come on, you guys, let's dance! I want to show you this cool move I learned from Ashley on the cheerleading squad!"

The pizza only took twenty minutes to arrive. For a few minutes, all the girls were quiet as they ate the delicious pizza.

"You guys! Can you believe we're in seventh grade

already?" Peichi broke the silence as she reached for a second piece. "It's nice not to be the babies of the school anymore. Now we're old enough to join the ski club, and take that cool class trip to Washington, D.C.!"

"What's everyone doing this year?" asked Shawn.

"You mean, for after-school activities?" asked Amanda. "For me, the school play, of course. If I make it, that is. The audition is Tuesday."

"Oh, you'll make it," Shawn assured her with a wave of her hand. "I want to do something along with cheerleading, but I don't know what. Molls, are you doing anything now, or will you just do softball next spring?"

Molly nodded as she chewed. "*Mmm-hmmm.*" She swallowed. "I want to do something new—something I've never done before! Maybe even a couple of new things."

Natasha poured herself some more soda. "I know what you mean, Molly. It would be fun to try something new. That's, like, the whole point of school!"

"Well, anyway," said Molly, "We all had amazing summers! Natasha went to the food and fashion capital of the world! Shawn was busting cool new moves in cheerleading camp, and Peichi got to visit ancient palaces in China! Amanda was becoming an amazing actress at Spotlight Arts Camp! I was a Super Sitter for two little kids on Cape Cod!"

The girls nodded, thinking back to their summer adventures and all the things they'd learned about themselves.

"And I think our amazing summer is gonna lead into our best year yet!" Molly went on. "...Windsor Middle School had better watch out! Right?"

"Woo-hoo!" cried the girls, reaching for a group high-five.

"There's no way I'm gonna wear that top, Manda."

"Oh, come on, Molls. It'll look so good on you!"

"You know I don't like pink...where's that long-sleeved striped T-shirt?"

Amanda rolled her eyes. "Not that shirt *again*, Molls! Come on—dress up for a change! We're going to a *party*—with eighth-graders!"

"I'll bet that you and Peichi and I are gonna be the only seventh-graders there," commented Molly. It was Saturday night, the night after the Browns' cooking job, and the twins were upstairs in the large bedroom they shared getting ready for a birthday party. Clothes were strewn across the beds, shoes spilled out of the twins' messy closet, and pop music blared from their clock radio.

"We're so cool, we've been invited to an eighth-grader's party!" joked Amanda. She was staring at her reflection in the twins' full-length mirror. "Are there gonna be boys there?"

Molly shrugged. "I don't know," she said. "But the entire girls' softball team is going." Athena Vardalos, the birthday girl, was the captain of Windsor Middle

School's girls' softball team, which Molly had joined last year. Athena had also been Molly's math tutor for most of sixth grade, and had helped Peichi for a bit, too.

"Can I do your hair?" Amanda asked Molly.

"Oh, Manda, this isn't a dance, it's just a birthday party."

Despite the fact that the twins both had long brown hair that turned reddish in the sun, green eyes, freckles, and long legs, their personalities were completely different. Molly, whose real name was Amelia, thought any hairstyle other than a ponytail was too much work. Amanda spent hours reading fashion magazines and playing with different looks. Molly wore stripes, Amanda wore glitter. But tonight, Amanda decided, she would make Molly glitter, too.

"Can I at least paint your nails?" she asked Molly.

Molly sighed. "I guess so."

"Yay!" said Amanda happily. "Tonight you're gonna have pretty nails!"

There was a knock at the door.

Molly opened the door to find her eight-year-old brother, Matthew, chewing a big wad of gum. "Whatcha doing?" he asked.

"Getting ready for a party."

"What time are ya coming home?"

"We're sleeping over at Peichi's after the party. What are you up to?"

"Watch this!" Matthew chewed his gum quickly,

then, with his eyes wide in concentration, blew a big pink bubble, which popped all over his pale freckled face.

"Hey, you finally did it!"

"Good job, Matthew," called Amanda. "You've finally learned how to blow a bubble!"

"I wanna watch myself in the mirror." Matthew squirmed past Molly, who tried to block him, and scrambled into the twins' adjoining bathroom that they had all to themselves—usually.

"Dad wants to know when you're gonna be ready, and if you're picking up Peichi," called Matthew from inside the big bathroom.

"Please tell him that we are *very* busy and *cannot* be rushed," said Amanda in a dramatic voice as she began to file Molly's stubby, broken nails.

"We'll be ready to go in twenty minutes," said Molly, making a funny face at Amanda. "And yes, we're picking up Peichi."

"Okay!" said Matthew as he ran out and tromped loudly down the stairs.

"Okay, now we soak your hands in a little bowl of water," said Amanda. "That's what they do at the nail salon." Sometimes Amanda went with Mom on Saturdays to get manicures. "I'll go get some." She went into the bathroom.

"*Aaaaaggh!*" she shrieked. "Oh, Matth-ewwww!"

When Molly ran into the bathroom, Amanda was

pointing at a gigantic green insect head and spiny legs peeking out from the shower curtain.

"Ha, ha," laughed Molly. "That's a good one! That rubber thing looks so real!"

"*Too* real," panted Amanda, her hand over her chest. "I'm gonna get him for that!"

Half an hour later, the twins stood before the mirror one more time. The September weather was still warm, so Amanda was wearing a denim dress with bangle bracelets. On her feet were cute red leather shoes with a square toe and a mary-jane strap. She'd blown all her Dish money on them. Her hair was parted on the side, the ends slightly curled with the curling iron. She'd finished the look with a touch of glitter on her bangs.

Molly's hair was in her favorite style, a high pony, but she'd let Amanda curl the ends so that they flipped up as one big curl. Molly had chosen red capris, a white sweater with short sleeves, and black sandals. She'd reached for the red shoes first, but Amanda pointed out that the red capris were enough. "Plus, your pants are a different shade of red than the shoes."

"Whatever," said Molly. "Let's grab Athena's gift and go! Peichi's gonna wonder what happened to us." Just then, the phone rang, and the twins laughed.

"Peichi," they said at the same time.

"Mol-ly! Aman-da! Ph-o-ne!" bellowed Matthew from the bottom of the stairs, which always drove Mom crazy. "It's Pei-chiiiii!"

"Tell her we're on our way, Matthew," said Amanda. "And come up and get your gross rubber bug before I throw it out the window."

"Ha, ha! I got you! Throw it down to me."

"No way! I'm not touching that thing."

"Hieeeee!" cried Peichi as she opened the car door. "Hi, Mr. Moore! This is gonna be fun! Do you guys like my top? It's my mom's but she accidentally washed it in hot water and it shrunk and she was so mad but she gave it to me and it fits me perfectly!"

She turned around to show the twins her white long-sleeved T-shirt, perfectly plain in front, but with a beautiful swirling design of small, emerald-green rhinestones on the back.

"Cool," said Molly as Peichi slipped into the car next to her, holding Athena's present.

"Very cool!" agreed Amanda. She looked at Dad, who was waiting patiently for Peichi to get settled, and said in a jokey British accent, "You may drive us to the party now,

Jeeves. Athena lives on President Street between Seventh and Eighth avenues."

"Certainly, madam," chuckled Mr. Moore. Five minutes later, they arrived at Athena's house. It looked a lot like the Moores' house on Taft Street—a dignified brick three-story townhouse with a colorful garden in the front.

"See you in the morning, Dad," said Molly.

"Bye, Dad," said Amanda.

"Bye, girls. Have fun!"

"Byeeee, Mr. Moore!" called Peichi. "Oh, hi, Athena!"

Athena stood at the front door. "Come on in!" she said. Her face was flushed with excitement, and her dark, wavy hair looked extra-shiny.

The girls came inside to find Athena's party in full swing, and it wasn't just for kids. Athena's grandparents, aunts, and uncles were there, too, talking and laughing with each other over loud pop music. A long table in the dining room was laden with tons of food. In a corner of the large living room, several tall, dark-haired girls who looked a lot like Athena were laughing and talking excitedly as they passed around a stack of snapshots.

"These are my cousins, who just got back from summer camp in Greece," Athena told the twins and Peichi. "Sondra, Christina...and my older sister, Rania. These are my friends, Molly, Amanda, and Peichi."

Everyone said hello, then Athena led the friends to the dining room.

"Help yourself," she said, pointing to the array of food.

"Wow!" exclaimed Peichi as her eyes scanned the table.

"This looks great!" said Molly, reaching for a plate. "What's that?" She pointed at a nearby dish.

"*Spanakopita.* You'll love it! It's spinach pie, a famous Greek dish. Here are *tiropites*—cheese appetizers—and over there is some *moussaka*—it has lamb, onions, tomatoes, cheese! Here are some sweets—*karithopita*, a walnut spice cake, and that's *baklava* over there, made with honey."

"*Mmmm,* honey," said Amanda, who loved sweets more than anyone.

"Have as much as you want—there's lots more food in the kitchen!"

Just then, an attractive woman with short dark hair and gold hoop earrings bustled over with a large wooden bowl in her hand. "Hello, girls! It's wonderful that you could join us!"

"This is my mom," said Athena. "Molly, Amanda, Peichi."

"It's nice to meet you," said the woman. Her dark eyes sparkled at the girls. "Molly, I remember you, of course, from softball. Please eat! We've been cooking for days!" She looked at the table and laughed. "Let's see if we can make some room for this salad!" Suddenly, the pop music was replaced by loud, lively music that sounded mostly like string instruments.

"Greek music," said Athena, groaning and grinning at the same time. "My dad just put it on! I knew he was gonna do this!"

"Turn it down, Nick!" called Mrs. Vardalos.

Standing near the stereo, a tall, handsome man with graying dark hair cupped his hand around his ear and called back, "What'd you say? Too loud?"

Mrs. Vardalos just shook her head, flashed a smile at the girls, and went to greet more relatives.

Once their plates were piled with food, Molly, Amanda, and Peichi sat down and ate with some other members of the softball team. All around them, everyone was laughing and talking.

"M*mmm*—I love this!" said Molly, as she ate a piece of spanakopita. "This pastry is so good, and the spinach inside has some nice seasonings in it."

"So does the moussaka," said Shawn.

"Come on, let's dance!" called Athena to the group of girls after a while. She beckoned for them to join her in the corner.

"Yeah, come on!" cried Peichi. "Wow, look at Athena's cousins dance! And her sister!"

The three older girls were shaking their shoulders to the music, and Christina was bending backward, lower and lower, until her shoulders touched the floor. Still shaking her shoulders, she gracefully came back up in time to the music.

"This is a great party!" Molly called to Athena.

"Thanks! Now you've seen my crazy family in action," said Athena with a grin.

The twins and Peichi loved dancing to the Greek music. As the music went faster and faster, the girls kept time—and whenever there was a loud clash of a tambourine, everyone whooped and clapped along. Some of the aunts and uncles joined in, crying, "Opa!"

"What does that mean?" Peichi wanted to know.

"It's a Greek word that means 'a zest for life'!"

"Opa!" shouted the Chef Girls, their faces bright red from dancing.

"Wow, I'm—hot," said Molly finally, and collapsed on the sofa, out of breath. The friends soon followed, and soon the only people left dancing were Rania, Sondra, and Christina, who switched the music back over to the pop station.

Mrs. Vardalos turned to a cluster of relatives who were laughing and clinking glasses. "Athena, time to open your gifts!"

The whole family watched as Athena opened her presents, *ooohing* and *aahing* along with Athena's friends at each CD, pair of earrings, book, or cute top.

"Oh!" said Peichi, checking her watch. "It's ten o'clock!" She went to the front door and spotted her dad's car. "Time to go," she told the twins.

"Thanks for coming!" said Athena, showing the friends to the door.

"We had a great time!" said the girls.

"And I want your mom's recipe for spana—spanakopita for the Dish cookbook," said Molly.

"You got it!"

A few minutes later, the girls were spreading out their sleeping bags in Peichi's large, airy living room. "My dad and I went to the video store and we rented three DVDs," Peichi said, giggling. "So we can stay up all night watching them, or watch one in the morning, or whatever!"

"Awesome! What'd you get?" Amanda asked as she pulled her oversized "Princess" nightshirt out of her backpack.

Just then, Mrs. Cheng passed by the living room. "Hello, girls," she said.

"Hi, Mrs. Cheng!" said the twins.

Mrs. Cheng looked like a model tonight, as usual. She was wearing pale-pink silk wide-legged pants, a matching tunic top, and white satin wedge slippers. Her short black bob haircut, parted in the middle, gleamed under the hall-way light. "I made you some popcorn for your movie marathon! And there's soda and juice in the fridge. Now, don't stay up *too* late, okay?" She winked at the girls as they giggled. "Good night," Mrs. Cheng called over her shoulder as she started up the stairs.

"Your mom looks like an actress in a movie," said Amanda. "You know, the old black-and-white kind where the ladies are always wearing, like, evening gowns, even when they go to bed or are making toast in the morning."

"Yeah," said Peichi. "And those are just her lounging clothes!" She giggled. "I'm still thirsty from all that dancing! What do you guys want to drink?"

"*Ooh*, I want root beer, please," Amanda said.

"Me, too!" chorused Molly. "No, wait, I want Coke!"

"Be right back," Peichi said as she hurried off to the kitchen. "Why don't you guys pick which movie you want to watch first?"

Molly flopped back onto her sleeping bag as Amanda walked over to the Chengs' big-screen TV to take a look at the DVDs. "I love sleeping over at Peichi's," Molly told her sister. "Her house is so—hey, what's that?"

"What's what?" asked Amanda, looking up.

"There are some books under here," Molly replied. "I hope no one's been looking for them!" She reached over and pulled the books out from under the couch as Amanda came over to see.

"City Baby," the twins read out loud, looking at the book jacket. It was a guide to having babies in New York City. There was another book underneath it.

"The Complete Baby Name Book," read Molly.

The twins looked at each other and did the twin thing: *Why are there baby books under the couch?*

Molly flipped to the back of *City Baby*. "This is a brand-new book," she said. She looked quizzically at Amanda.

"Well—" began Amanda. "Uh, then these aren't books from when Peichi was born."

The twins looked at each other again and said with their eyes, *These books are being hidden!*

"Oh, now I feel like I'm spying!" said Molly. She quickly shoved the books back under the couch with a guilty expression on her face.

"Hi! Which movie did you pick?" Peichi asked, bringing in a tray of drinks. Both twins jumped.

"Uh, we couldn't decide," fibbed Molly. She stood up. "Let's watch whatever you want."

As Peichi set up the movie, Molly felt like she'd burst with what she was thinking. So she said in a casual tone, "Hey, Peichi, do you ever wish you had, like, a baby brother or sister?"

Peichi shrugged. "Not really. I think it would be fun to have a twin, though!"

Amanda flashed Molly a look that said, *You and your big mouth!* But Molly didn't see it.

"Why do you ask, anyway?" Peichi asked Molly.

"Oh, I don't know...but, well, there are some new books over here about what to name your baby and stuff."

"Huh?" asked Peichi. "Where?"

"They're, um, under the couch," Molly replied uncomfortably.

"Nice going, Molls," muttered Amanda. "You shouldn't have said that."

Peichi found the books. "That's weird," she said. "Oh, I know! My mom designs book jackets sometimes, for a big publishing company. Maybe that's what these are…" But she didn't sound too sure.

Molly swallowed hard. She was beginning to wish she hadn't said anything. And Amanda was glaring at her. "Oh, that's it," Molly said lightly. "I mean, she probably just wanted to see what the jackets looked like when the books came out."

"Yeah," Peichi said slowly. "Well…let's start the movie."

Me and my big mouth, thought Molly. *It was none of my business to say something like that…or to get out those books in the first place!* She was glad that the girls could watch movies for the rest of the sleepover. Having the TV on helped cover the awkwardness.

For hours that night, each girl pretended to be asleep.

I'm such a jerk, Molly told herself as she stared into the dark.

I hope I do well at the audition, thought Amanda, shifting restlessly.

What's going on around here? fretted Peichi, biting her lip. *And when is anyone gonna tell me anything?*

The next morning, as the first light came in through the big picture windows, Molly turned her head to look at Amanda.

Amanda, who'd been staring up at the ceiling, rolled over toward her sister. "You're awake," she whispered to Molly.

"Yeah."

Peichi stirred, then groaned. "I'm awake, too," she said. "I don't know if I slept at all!"

Molly sat up. "I think I want to head home. Peichi, is it okay if we don't stay for breakfast?"

"It's okay," said Peichi with a nod. She seemed sort of relieved.

"It's just that we're wide awake, and we might as well get going."

After having a glass of orange juice with Peichi in the kitchen, the twins made the short walk home.

"You girls are up early!" called Dad, who'd just opened the door to get the newspaper.

"We didn't want to miss your pancakes, Dad!" Molly called back with a wave.

Meanwhile, Peichi sat in the quiet

kitchen, flipping through a catalog as she waited for her parents to get up. *Should I ask them what's going on?* she wondered, as she traced her finger around the red rooster design on her juice glass. *Wait a minute—this is all ridiculous. Mom's not having another baby. She just isn't. Maybe those books are a present for someone else! Somebody who is having a baby!*

And she put the entire thing out of her mind.

For about three minutes.

Breakfast that morning at the Chengs' was ordinary enough. As the three ate scrambled eggs and talked together, Peichi closely watched her parents' faces for clues—but she had to admit to herself that they weren't acting different. They asked her about Athena's party, and how much homework she had left to do. They talked about the yard work they planned to do all day. *They're acting completely normal,* Peichi thought. *Those books have to be a present for somebody else. I wonder who's pregnant!*

Near the end of breakfast, Peichi was too curious to hold it in any longer. She blurted out, "So, who's having a baby?"

Mr. Cheng choked on his coffee, and Mrs. Cheng reached over to pat him on the back. They glanced at each other, surprised, and Mr. Cheng cleared his throat.

"How—how do you know?" he asked Peichi.

"I saw the baby books under the couch," Peichi replied as her heart began to pound. "What's going on?"

"There's something we'd like to talk to you about, Pom-Pom," began Mrs. Cheng.

Pom-Pom? She hasn't called me that in, like, four years, thought Peichi.

Mrs. Cheng looked over at her husband, then turned to Peichi. "We are soon going to have some—changes around here."

"Like what?" asked Peichi. Her mouth felt completely dry, so she reached for her juice.

"Big changes," replied Mr. Cheng with a broad smile.

"Well, I'm—expecting a baby," announced Mrs. Cheng. "You're going to be a big sister, Peichi—in about six more months!"

Peichi gulped. She gripped the sides of her chair to steady herself. Suddenly, she felt like everything in her life, this house, had—shifted. Changed forever.

Who are these people?

"Really?" was all she could think to say as her parents watched for her reaction. "Why?"

"Why?" echoed her parents. They glanced at each other.

"Why do you want to have another baby?" asked Peichi. "It's been just the three of us for so long."

"We thought four would be even nicer," said Mr. Cheng. "Don't you?"

"Well, uh—" Peichi began. Suddenly an image came to her of a cute, chubby baby with black hair and dark eyes...drinking from a bottle, standing with wobbly knees as she stood over him, holding his tiny hands...she had to smile at the thought.

"You'll be a wonderful big sister," said Mrs. Cheng, stroking Peichi's cheek. "Just think how nice it'll be to have a baby in the house! You'll sing to the baby and play funny little games. You'll have a relationship with your little brother or sister that you've never had before. You won't be an only child anymore!"

Peichi began to relax as she thought of Molly and Amanda and the special bond they shared with each other, and with Matthew. The twins taught him things. They protected him. They laughed and joked and squabbled and goofed around and played at the beach with him. Even though Matthew could sometimes be a pain, he was—a part of them. And they would always be connected.

Now she'd know what all of that would be like.

Except...

"But I'll be so much older than the baby," Peichi pointed out. "It's not like with the twins, or even the twins with Matthew. It's not like we'll ever be in the same school at the same time, or—"

"That's true," said Mr. Cheng. "But think about how the baby will look up to you. And you can watch him or her grow up!"

Peichi looked down at the polished wooden floor. She felt like crying, but she felt like jumping up and down, too. Something exciting and amazing was going to happen! Something new and different! What would it all be like?

And yet things would never, ever be the same...

Mrs. Cheng seemed to read Peichi's thoughts. She took Peichi's hand. "Life is all about change," she told her. "It never stays the same. It shouldn't! That's what makes life so exciting and wonderful."

Mr. Cheng tapped Peichi under her chin, something he'd always done to make her smile. "You'll always be our precious Peichi," he told her. "That's one thing that'll never change."

Peichi took a deep breath as she smiled at her parents. "Well. It'll be cool to have a brother or a sister. And some-day, we can take the baby to China!"

"I'm glad you feel that way, sweetheart," said Mr. Cheng, as he and Mrs. Cheng smiled with relief.

"Do Ah-mah and Ah-yeh know yet?" asked Peichi. She was speaking of Mr. Cheng's parents, who lived in Chinatown in Manhattan, a short subway ride away.

"Not yet! We wanted you to be the first to know," said Mrs. Cheng.

"They're going to be so surprised," said Peichi, her old enthusiasm returning. "I can't wait to tell them! Let's call them right now!"

While Peichi and her parents were telling their exciting news to Ah-mah and Ah-yeh, the phone rang at the Moores' house, where the twins were sitting together in the kitchen. For once, Molly picked it up before Amanda had a chance to.

"Hello, Molly?" said a boy's voice on the line.

Whoa—it's Justin! Molly thought as her heart started to pound. Justin had been Amanda's longtime crush—until the twins found out that he liked Molly. It had made for an uncomfortable situation between the girls when they returned from their summers away. During the summer, both Molly and Justin had been on Cape Cod, where Justin's family vacationed each year. Molly had gone there to work as a mother's helper for the Brewsters, who lived next door to the Moores. She and Justin had hung out a lot and had had a great time together. They had become good friends—but for Justin, it had turned into something more. Molly had been completely surprised when Justin gave her a bracelet on his last day on the Cape.

Amanda had had a hard time dealing with it all when she found out, and while things were better now, the tension wasn't completely gone. Only Shawn knew what had happened—and Mom, of course.

"Uh—hi, what's up?" asked Molly cautiously. She didn't want Amanda to know that Justin was on the line. The twins had been through enough already!

"Guess what," replied Justin cheerfully. "I found out that I'm gonna be the Sports photo editor on *The Post* this year! I got promoted! Isn't that cool?"

"Oh, that's—good," replied Molly in a businesslike tone. She turned her head ever so slightly in Amanda's direction. As she'd feared, Amanda was giving her that questioning look that meant, *Who's calling?*

Molly shrugged helplessly, as if to reply, *I don't have anything to do with this.*

It's Justin! Amanda realized, her mouth going dry. *And he's not calling for me.* Suddenly, she felt like an outsider. She wanted to leave the kitchen, but her legs didn't seem to work. She sat, frozen, her eyes locked on the floor. *Justin's calling for Molly! He doesn't even want to talk to me! I'm so glad I didn't pick up the phone.*

"Listen," said Molly just then, interrupting Justin as he went on about his promotion. "I have to go baby-sit now. I'll—uh—talk to you later. Bye." She hung up, then looked at Amanda.

"Manda, I have to run next door," said Molly. "I'm late."

"Uh, all right. Have fun baby-sitting." Amanda forced a smile. She was bummed about the call, but she knew she really couldn't be mad at Molly. It wasn't Molly's fault that Justin had a crush on her.

"Do you want to come over there later?" asked Molly.

"Uh, yeah, maybe."

"Okay."

Molly ran upstairs to brush her teeth and put on her shoes. *I hung up so fast with him,* she thought. *I hope I didn't hurt his feelings! It's really cool that Justin's Sports photo editor now...he deserves it.* For a moment, she paused as she put on her shoe. She was realizing something—that she was happy he'd called to tell her his good news.

She stood up, went to the dresser, and opened a low drawer.

Molly reached under a pile of old t-shirts, and pulled out a small box that contained the pretty bracelet, made of tiny polished pink shells, that Justin had given her.

Molly stared at the bracelet. It brought the summer back in a rush—the sound of the waves, the cool, fresh ocean breezes, the feel of the hot sand under her feet as she played volleyball with Justin...

Then, with a sigh, she tucked the box into its hiding place and quietly closed the drawer.

Justin and I can't be friends. We just can't.

She quickly brushed her teeth, and ran downstairs and next door to the Brewsters.

Half an hour later, Amanda went upstairs to the twins' cluttered room. With a smile, she realized that it was mostly her stuff that took up the space.

Mom and Dad and Matthew were still at Matthew's soccer game. She felt lonely all by herself in the big house, even though Molly was just next door.

Amanda flopped down on her bed, and her mind turned back to the phone call. *Justin likes Molly, not you. Justin likes Molly, not you. Justin likes...*

Amanda sat up quickly, fighting the urge to feel sorry for herself.

I know! she thought suddenly. *I'll go through our clothes and pick out the ones that don't fit anymore. Mom wants to donate them to charity, and she's been bugging us about it forever!*

Feeling a burst of energy, Amanda got right to work, beginning with the dresser. It didn't take long until she uncovered a small box under a pile of old T-shirts.

What's this? she wondered. She opened it and found the pink shell bracelet.

Oh, great. This is just what I needed to find right now—another reminder! No matter what I do, I can't get away from it—Justin likes Molly, not me.

*A*manda stared at the bracelet. *Maybe Molly really does like Justin. Maybe she takes this out every day and looks at it...*

And Justin had just called. Had Molly known he would?

Amanda sat on her bed. Then she stood up and placed the box back in its hiding place.

She sat down again, staring at herself in the big mirror. Just then, some clouds covered the sun, and the twins' room got suddenly dark.

Amanda sighed. *Come on*, she told herself. *You and Molly have worked through this already.*

A few weeks ago, when Molly had told Amanda about the bracelet, and that she and Justin had hung out so much together, Amanda had felt betrayed—even though Molly had insisted that she didn't like Justin. After getting some good advice from Shawn, Amanda had realized that even though she felt bad now, someday it would all be okay.

But when?

A few minutes later, Amanda went outside to the garden. She could hear Molly playing with little Nathan and baby Charlotte in the Brewsters' garden.

"Molls?" she called as she stood by the fence.

"Hi, Manda," Molly called back.

"Can I come over?"

"Sure, I'll let you in."

Amanda wrote a quick note to her parents telling them where she was, then headed next door.

Molly was waiting at the front door with Charlotte in her arms. "Let's go back outside," she said.

As the girls played trucks with Nathan, and Charlotte watched from her playpen, Molly said, "What's up, Manda? You look—upset."

Amanda tried to smile, but she knew it wasn't working. "It's just that—I was cleaning out the dresser? You know, 'cause Mom asked us to?"

Molly's face clouded over.

"...And I found the box," Amanda continued. "With the bracelet in it. And—I don't know, it just got me feeling kinda down, and, you know, wondering if maybe you really *do* like Justin? I was—just wondering."

"Where's the yellow truck?" asked Nathan.

Molly quickly passed it to him, then sighed. "I don't like Justin, Manda. I've told you that before."

"Well, do you—like having the bracelet? I mean, like, are you gonna wear it to school, where he'll see it?"

Molly shrugged. "I don't know. I don't know what to do with it!" She smiled at her sister, hoping to lighten the mood. "You know I'm not really into jewelry."

As sad as she felt, Amanda had to smile back. "I know. Well, I'm gonna head back and keep cleaning."

"Okay. I'll walk you out...Um, Manda? I won't be friends with Justin. I already decided that. Okay?"

Amanda paused at the door. "Um, well—okay..." She paused.

"Molly?" called Nathan from the garden. "Come back, Molly!"

"I'll see you later," said Amanda quickly, so that Molly could get back to the kids.

Back at home, Amanda was alone again. She plopped into Dad's beat-up leather armchair. *When is everyone coming home?* she wondered. Molly's words echoed in her head. "...I won't be friends with Justin..."

But something about that didn't seem right.

Deep down, a tiny voice seemed to ask Amanda, *Do you really want to control who Molly is friends with?*

Well, do you?

At dinner that night, the twins were a little quiet. Matthew was quick to take advantage of his big sisters' silence.

"So, everyone, guess what's coming up really soon! Well, not *really* soon, but kinda soon!"

No one said anything.

"My birthday!"

"Oh, right!" said Mom, with a twinkle in her eye. *She* hadn't really forgotten.

"Did you guys forget?"

"Of course not, Matthew," said Amanda, pouring him some more milk. "Your birthday's around Halloween. We can't think of Halloween without thinking of your birthday."

"Do you want a party this year, Matthew?" asked Mom.

"Yeah!" replied Matthew. "A cool party."

Molly brightened. "Let's make a haunted house for your party this year! In the basement!"

"Ooooh!" cried Matthew. "Can we, Mom? Can I have a haunted house birthday party?"

"Well, as long as it's not too scary," said Mom.

"Great idea!" agreed Amanda. "We could make really cool food for it!"

"Like what?" asked Matthew.

"Oh, like chocolate spiders and—I don't know, all kinds of funny stuff. We'll find lots of ideas on the Internet."

"I'll bet the Chef Girls would help us," said Molly.

"Especially if you pay them," cracked Matthew.

"We'll help, too," said Dad. His blue eyes twinkled behind his glasses as he grinned at the kids. "I love this kind of thing! Lumber yard, here I come!"

"Uh-oh," groaned Mom in a jokey voice. "I think there's going to be some noisy hammering and sawing going on pretty soon."

"Woo-hoo!" cried the kids. Dad was good at building things—their haunted house was going to be so great!

After dinner, the twins logged on the computer in the den. "Let's type in 'Halloween parties' and see what we get," suggested Molly.

It didn't take long for the girls to find some great ideas.

"Look at this!" exclaimed Molly. "Chocolate 'bat' cake. That looks so easy!"

"That's really fun," said Amanda. "Matthew and his friends are gonna love it. Great, let's bookmark that page...done." Then she clicked the "Back" button. "Now let's see what we can find for the haunted house!"

"I know! Let's have one room in the haunted house where we lead the kids, and they have to touch icky things," suggested Molly. "They'll have to wear a blind-fold, and we can make stuff like cold spaghetti—and they'll have to reach down into the bowl—and we'll have gross stuff in it!"

"Like 'eyeballs' that we can make from—I don't know, grapes or something!" added Amanda.

The twins laughed, then Molly grew quickly serious.

"Manda," she said. "About today—uh, the Justin thing—I'm sorry—"

"Molly," interrupted Amanda. "Listen. I don't think you should have to—to not talk to him anymore or anything like that. That wouldn't be fair. It would be ridiculous, actually! Because, like, we're all in this group of friends, and we're in the same school, and there's no way to avoid him, anyway!"

Molly nodded. "Well, that's true. But are you okay if Justin and I stay friends?"

Amanda nodded. "I will be. It might take a little while. But you're more important to me than any dumb boy." She smiled. "You know what Aunt Livia told me once? 'Boys come and go, but sisters are forever.'"

"That's for sure!" said Molly. "And there are a lot of dumb boys out there." The twins laughed, and Amanda felt freer and a lot less lonely than she had earlier that day.

"Let's send a funny e-mail to the Chef Girls," suggested Molly. "A mysterious one about helping us with the party."

"I wonder if we can make it rhyme?" asked Amanda. "Let's try."

So after a lot of typing—and a lot of laughing!—the twins had written:

44

To: happyface; qtpie490; BrooklynNatasha
From: mooretimes2
Re: :-o   :-o

Something very spooky must be done
For a freckle-faced kid's birthday fun.
Do you have the GUTS to be scary and icky?
Then help us make things gooey and sticky!
There will be screams
and frights galore,
And we'll leave the
little goblin wanting more!
Heh heh heh
OOOOHHHH!
Meet us in the hall tomorrow morning
IF YOU DARE
And we'll tell you what we're gonna do
for a scare!
Ha ha ha ha ha ha ha ha!!!!!

The twins had so much fun writing their poem that at one point, Dad stuck his head into the den. "What's so funny?" he asked. "I heard you laughing all the way upstairs."

"Look at our poem! Isn't it good?" said the twins.

Dad's eyes crinkled as he read. "Excellent work," he said, chuckling. "Now off to bed."

That night after Molly turned off the light, Amanda said, "Molls? What are you gonna dress up as for Matthew's party?"

"*Mmmph*...I dunno...maybe you," said Molly. "Night."

"Hey, that's actually pretty funny," said Amanda. "And I'll be you!"

The next morning, the twins met up with Peichi, Shawn, and Natasha before school and told them about the haunted house.

"Sounds like fun," said Shawn. "I'm in."

"Good," said Molly. "We need your artistic skills!"

"I'll help, too," said Natasha.

"What about you, Peichi?" asked Amanda. "Uh, Peichi?"

"Oh!" said Peichi, who shook herself out of a daydream. "Sorry. Sure. Whatever."

"Is everything okay, Peichi?" asked Shawn, giggling. "Usually it's Molly who spaces out."

"Well, yeah! Something big is happening. At home." Peichi smiled. "We're sort of getting—an addition."

"You're putting in a tennis court!" said Shawn breathlessly.

"No," giggled Peichi. "Where would we put a tennis—"

"A *baby!*" shouted the twins. "Your mom is having a baby!"

Shawn and Natasha looked at each other as if to say, *What gave the twins that idea?*

"Yeah! Isn't that, uh, cool? I mean, I'm still kinda getting used to the idea that we're gonna have a baby in the house!

Things are gonna be so different. But that's good! Right?"

"Wow, Peichi, that's so cool," said Shawn.

"I wish I was getting a little brother or sister!" Natasha exclaimed.

As the bell rang, the Chef Girls hurried off to home-room. *Everyone thinks having a new baby in the family will be awesome*, Peichi thought. *I hope they're right!*

The Chef Girls had trouble concentrating in school that day. All were thinking about Peichi's huge news. It was wild to think that in just a few months, there would be a brand-new little *person* at the Chengs' house!

There was other stuff to think about, too, like new classes. French class! Spanish class! Home Economics class—which, for the Chef Girls, was going to be a breeze... and, of course, deciding which after-school activities to sign up for. All the girls agreed that the start of the school year was the most fun!

"Nice work, Amelia," said Ms. Rand, handing Molly's essay to her later that afternoon in English class.

"Thanks, Ms. Rand. Um, you can call me Molly."

"That's right, I forgot. Anyway, your essay on what life

would be like in the year 2025 was very interesting—and entertaining, too! I loved the part about the self-cleaning house. Do you enjoy writing?"

Molly blushed, because half the class was listening. She shrugged. "I guess so. It *is* kind of fun to make stuff up and put it in a story!"

After class, Natasha followed Molly into the hall. "I heard what Ms. Rand said about your writing," she told Molly. "Can I read your paper?"

"Sure," said Molly, handing the paper to her.

"I think you should write for *The Post*," suggested Natasha. "Why don't you come with me to the next meeting? It would be fun."

"*The Post,*" mused Molly. "*Hmm.*"

"You said you wanted to try new things," Natasha reminded her. "Remember? Well, this is your chance. See you later!" She headed to Science class.

As Molly walked into study hall, she pictured herself typing up fascinating articles just before the deadline... seeing kids reading her stories, pointing to her name below the headline...attending meetings with Natasha and—

Wait a minute. I can't join The Post. *Justin's on* The Post! *That would be like rubbing it in Amanda's face. And maybe he would make a big deal about sitting next to me at the meetings...how embarrassing. Oh, brother. Is this never gonna end?*

Molly smiled and shook her head as she pictured herself avoiding Justin through the rest of middle school, and then high school...and maybe even college!

That evening, Molly and Mom happened to be alone in the kitchen after dinner. Molly told her about her dilemma. "Can I join *The Post,* or should I *not* join, because of Amanda and the whole Justin thing?"

Mom put down the sponge she was cleaning the counter with. "Is writing on *The Post* something you'd really like to do? Or do you want to join because Justin is involved with it?" she asked.

Molly wrinkled her nose. "Mo-o-m! I'm not gonna join a club because some *boy* is in it! I just think it would be fun. I'm ready to try some different things."

"Then you should do it," stated Mom. "Amanda will get used to the situation, don't worry."

Molly smiled and shrugged. "I *guess* she will. But I'm almost afraid to tell her about it!"

Mom laughed. "You're both young. This Justin thing will pass," she assured Molly. "Join *The Post* if you want to write."

As the twins walked to school the next morning, Molly cleared her throat and said, "You know, I think I might go to the next *Post* meeting with Natasha. Just to check it out."

"Oh, really?" asked Amanda. "Huh." As Molly watched her anxiously, Amanda looked away for a moment.

Uh-oh, thought Molly, her hand clutching at the hem of her jacket. *Here it comes.*

But Amanda turned back to Molly with a smile. "Go for it," she said. "It'll be awesome to see articles you wrote in the paper!"

Amanda had more important things on her mind than boys who didn't like her, anyway. The auditions for the fall play were being held that day—and despite the fact that she'd been in plays before and performed well at Spotlight, she was nervous.

It was hard not to be, since Ms. Barlow, who directed the plays and taught drama, was also Amanda's French teacher. BE A STAR! PLAY AUDITIONS TUESDAY—COME OUT AND AUDITION! screamed the chalkboard in her class-room. Amanda was distracted by the notice for the entire class.

After the bell rang, Amanda handed Ms. Barlow a videotape cassette.

"Here's my performance tape from Spotlight, Ms. Barlow," she said. "I hope you like it! My scene went really well that last night. I wish you could've been there!"

"*Won*-derful!" exclaimed Ms. Barlow, her mascaraed brown eyes widening as she reached for the cassette. "I look forward to seeing you do your star turn in the *round,* before such a *large* audience!" She beamed at Amanda as she slid the tape into her big leather tote. "See you this afternoon at the audition!"

Just a few hours later, Amanda was sitting in the vast auditorium, nervously tapping her foot. She knew she'd be called up to the stage any moment. Her hands trembled as she held the script she was to read, but her eyes were fixed on a tall girl onstage who spoke the lines as if she were living them.

"Thank you kindly, Colonel Bryant," the girl said to the boy reading with her. She did a little curtsey—which might have looked silly if someone else had tried it just for an audition, but looked perfectly natural when she did it. She didn't seem nervous at all—in fact, she commanded the stage. Her long, copper-colored hair gleamed, and everything about her seemed graceful and relaxed. Every kid in the audience was watching her closely, Amanda realized. For once, there was no whispering or the rattling of scripts anywhere in the auditorium.

Wow! thought Amanda enviously. *This girl's only in the sixth grade? She's so—amazing up there! Boy, am I gonna have some serious competition this year.*

"...That was just *wonderful*—thank you, Becca!" called

Ms. Barlow. Becca Mooney flashed a confident smile and quickly exited the stage, her audition over.

There was a pause.

Not me not yet not me not yet, reeled Amanda's thoughts.

"Amanda Moore, go on up, please!"

Oh, great! Why do I have to follow the amazing sixth-grader?

Meanwhile, Molly was about to attend her first *Post* meeting. She'd met up with Natasha after school, and they'd run into Justin in the hall on the way there.

"Hi, Molly! Are you going to the meeting?" he exclaimed. He seemed to light up at the thought of Molly joining *The Post.* It *was* kind of funny and cute, Molly thought.

But I'm not gonna sit next to him, she decided as the three walked into the small newspaper office. Molly quickly found a chair next to the wall, and gave Natasha a look that said, *Sit next to me!*

But Natasha was greeting a fellow "Postie," and didn't see Molly's look. Justin grabbed the seat.

Molly suddenly felt a little more—alive with Justin there. Or was she just excited about trying something new?

Just then, a dark-haired eighth grade girl walked in and took a seat at the big desk that faced the room.

"That's our new editor-in-chief," Justin whispered to Molly. "The editor-in-chief is always an eighth-grader, who's chosen at the end of seventh grade."

"Hi," said the girl, looking at Molly. "I'm Liza Pedersen."

"Hi, I'm Molly Moore."

"You're new to *The Post*, right?"

The *Post* staff all turned to look at Molly. She felt her cheeks burn.

"Uh-huh. I thought I'd come and—check it out."

"Great! We're glad you're here. I'm sure we'll find lots for you to do!"

By the end of the meeting, several writing and photography assignments had been handed out, and Molly, who'd told Liza she'd be happy to write any kind of article, had been asked to cover the next meeting of the Windsor Volunteers' Club.

"The club is a fairly new one," Liza told Molly. "I think more students should hear about it. Please write a short article about what the club is all about, what their upcoming projects are, that sort of thing. Okay?"

"Okay," said Molly, scribbling down notes.

She was beginning to feel like a reporter already!

Back in the auditorium, Amanda inhaled sharply as she stood up. She walked toward the steps that led to the stage.

Don't trip, she thought, picturing herself falling flat on her face in front of the whole auditorium of kids.

"We'll do the flashback Civil War scene. Ready?" called Ms. Barlow.

"Ready!" Amanda called back from center stage.

"Brett, please start," called Ms. Barlow.

Brett McClelland, a seventh-grader new to Windsor Middle School, looked down at his script. "Mrs. Lucille Cavendish, I'm Colonel Bryant. I have news—about your husband Winston."

"Wh-what is it?" read Amanda. "Is it—bad?" Her character, a Southern Civil War wife, was supposed to be upset and worried.

"Your husband is in a military hospital near Shelbyville," continued Brett. "He's been seriously injured, ma'am. But we found this letter in his pocket. It's addressed to you."

"Please let me see it. Oh, thank you, Colonel Bryant. When can I go to him?" There! Amanda had nailed it. She sounded perfectly upset without being fake. *My Southern accent isn't too bad, either,* she congratulated herself, grateful that she'd taken a dialect workshop at camp where she'd learned how to speak with several different accents.

Amanda took a deep breath, faced the auditorium full of faces, and read, "This has been a long and terrible war, Colonel Bryant. The South will never be the same again. Do—do you think this war will end soon?"

"Thank you, Amanda!" called Ms. Barlow.

That's it? Already?

"Okay," called Amanda, as she turned to leave the stage. "Thank you."

That was fast. I hardly got to read anything! Amanda thought as she carefully walked down the steps and up the aisle, her heart pounding. But more kids than usual had turned out for the audition, she realized, passing row after row of hopefuls. *Ms. Barlow's probably in a hurry to get through everybody.*

Plus, she already knows what I can do, Amanda reminded herself. *That's why I didn't need much time!*

After the audition, Amanda headed home, her mind deep in happy thoughts. *I hope I get the part of Lucille,* she thought, picturing herself in a hoop skirt. *The costumes for this play are going to be amazing! I'd love to wear a long silk dress in emerald green, just like Scarlett O'Hara's in* Gone With the Wind...

"Hey, Amanda! Wait up," called a familiar voice. Amanda spun around.

Ohmigosh! It's Justin!

Amanda's heart began to pound, just as it had in the auditorium. "Oh, hi. What's up?" she said, trying to sound casual.

Justin started walking with Amanda. "Not much! What are you up to?"

Why do you want to know? "Oh, not much...um, I just finished auditioning for the play."

Justin's grin seemed genuine. "That's cool! You're a shoo-in, Amanda. You'll probably be the star of the play this year!"

Amanda laughed, embarrassed. "Oh, I don't know..."

There was a pause.

"So," Justin said, "How's seventh grade going so far? Too bad we're not in any classes together."

Huh?

"I heard you were in Mr. Garcia's science class," continued Justin. "Is he tough? I have Ms. Feldman. She's not too bad."

How do you know I'm in Mr. Garcia's class? Amanda wanted to ask. She liked that Justin knew something about her she hadn't told him herself. But then she realized, *Oh, Molly must have mentioned it. That's all.* "He's okay," replied Amanda. "But he gives a ton of home-work. And we have a quiz tomorrow."

"So do I," groaned Justin. "In four different classes! Well, I'm going this way." He pointed to Fourth Street.

"I'm heading over to Omar's house. See ya! I hope you find your name on the big board tomorrow morning—as the star of the play. Then I'll get to photograph you again for the paper!"

Amanda laughed despite herself, as she got caught up in Justin's enthusiasm. "Uh, thanks. I guess I'll see you tomorrow, maybe."

"Right! Bye." Justin waved and headed across the street.

Wow! thought Amanda. *He was so—nice. I wonder if maybe—just maybe—there's still a chance that Justin likes me...just a little. Oh, I hope he does...*

The next morning, Amanda and Molly squeezed their way into the cluster of kids who stood before Ms. Barlow's "big board," which listed the names of the students who'd made the audition for *An American Journey.*

Amanda's eyes quickly scanned the list. *Becca Mooney—of course!* Amanda thought...*Edward Ling... Veera Tashjian...*

Wait a minute. Where's my name?

Her heart seemed to skip.

Calm down, she told herself, *you just missed it.*

But the anxious look on Molly's face fueled Amanda's fears. The twins looked up and down the list one more time—then Molly silently guided Amanda through the jostling, shrieking crowd to a quiet corner at the end of the hall.

"I didn't make it," said Amanda, dazed. "Right? I didn't make it."

"I'm sorry, Manda. That really stinks. You said you did so well!"

"I—I *did* do well! At least, I thought I did."

Didn't I?

59

A few hours later, Molly sighed heavily as she turned a page in her notebook. Half the kids in study hall turned to look at her.

Yipes, thought Molly. *That was loud.* But she couldn't help it—she knew exactly what her twin was feeling right now, down the hall.

In Ms. Barlow's French class.

How awful it must be, thought Molly, as she tried to focus on the notes before her. *Poor Manda has to see Ms. Barlow every day—what a horrible reminder that she didn't make the play!*

Molly read a few lines of her Social Studies notes from the morning, then realized she hadn't taken in the information at all. She reread them.

FOR NEXT TUESDAY:

Write a paper on any social issue.

Pick something I'm interested in.

Talk about the problems / what's being done

to solve the problems + my own ideas

to make things better.

Molly's heart still felt heavy for Amanda, but she slowly began to focus on her homework. *This sounds like a cool assignment,* she thought. *But what social issue should I pick?*

Molly found her answer later that afternoon, as she sat in the cafeteria with the members of the Windsor Volunteers' Club. There weren't many—only three people had shown up.

One of them was Elizabeth, who was looking for a new activity since she'd injured herself at cheerleading camp over the summer. "Now that I won't be able to cheer, I thought this would be good for me to do," she told Molly. "Maybe helping other people will keep me from feeling too sorry for myself."

A slender, dark-haired girl cleared her throat just then, and said, "Hi, everyone. I'm Karen Woo, and I started this club last year. I'm glad you're here! And I'm excited to announce that we're going to be part of something really cool! It's a biggie—a charity harvest fair at Prospect Park in mid-October. All the money we raise will go to America's Second Harvest. That's an

61

organization that operates food banks and distributes food to the hungry."

That's it! Molly's eyes brightened as she had an idea. *Hunger—that's the social issue I could write about for Social Studies! Okay, that's figured out. Now start thinking like a reporter.* Molly cleared her throat. "Karen, do you mean that you'll have a booth at the fair?" she asked.

Karen nodded. "That's right. We'll sell baked goods, maybe cider, that kind of thing. But I'm not sure we can do it alone. We could use some other sponsors... after all, we have to pay for the booth, set it up and decorate it, publicize the fair, get people to bake stuff, organize games and prizes, find volunteers to run the booth..."

That sounds fun—and different, thought Molly. *I'll do more than just report on this club—I'll join it. Getting people to bake stuff will be easy...I'm gonna talk to the Chef Girls about this! I hope they'll all sign on to cook...and work on this project with me.*

That evening wasn't the most pleasant one at the Moores'. Matthew had the stomach flu, and Amanda was still devastated about not getting a role in the play. She kept fighting back tears at the dinner table.

"I know how upset you must be, honey," said Mom sympathetically. "But maybe Ms. Barlow wanted to give some other kids a chance. Is it a small cast?"

"Pretty small," replied Amanda. "It's just that I feel so stupid—I mean, practically the whole school knows I just got back from drama camp! It's *so* embarrassing!"

"Maybe it'll help if you talk to Ms. Barlow," suggested Dad. "I'm sure she'll explain why she made the choice that she did." Mom and Molly nodded.

Amanda sighed. "Well, I see her every day in French class. I guess I could talk to her. But right now I don't even want to *see* her. Today was so hard in her class—I avoided her, actually."

"We're just proud that you tried out, sweetheart," said Mom. "You took a chance. That's how you've gotten in the plays before, and don't worry—you'll be in other plays. Hey, why don't you still work on the play? Maybe sign up for costume crew? You love fashion, and I think you'd have a lot of fun with that."

Amanda rolled her eyes, then saw Molly giving her "the look." This time, "the look" meant, *Don't be rude to Mom like that!*

"Sorry, Mom," Amanda said quickly. "It's not a bad idea—but—you know, I just...I can't imagine being that close to the play, and not onstage." She twirled her spaghetti around her fork and sighed. "I need to think about it.

"So, Molls, what did you do today?" asked Dad.

Molly told the family all about the Volunteers' Club and the charity harvest fair. "I'm really excited about it!" she added. "Amanda, do you want to do it with me? I'm gonna try to get all the Chef Girls involved. And Elizabeth's doing it, too. She joined the club."

Amanda shrugged. "I'll definitely have the time, since I won't be busy with the play."

"More garlic bread, anyone?" asked Dad brightly, trying to lighten the mood. "Molls, you've got some interesting stuff going on. I think you're going to like reporting for *The Post.*"

"Me, too," said Molly. She smiled at her parents. "I said I wanted to try some different things, and I am! I think I even feel a little different already!"

"Well, you *look* completely different—oh, wait, that's Amanda," Dad teased her. "Here, help me finish up this salad. You, too, Manda. *Mmm*—I love your mom's Caesar salad!"

After the twins helped Mom with the dishes, Molly settled herself in front of the computer and got to work on her article. *Let's see,* she thought. *I guess I'll start with the headline. The headlines in* The Post *always sound catchy...*

These are so blah! she thought. She headed back to the kitchen, where Dad and Mom were sipping tea and paying bills.

"Why don't you put a food pun in the headline?" Dad suggested as he looked at Molly's paper. "Like 'dish up' or something?"

Molly brightened. "Oh, that's great!" She thought for a moment. "Like, 'Windsor Volunteers Serve Up Harvest for the Hungry'?" She giggled.

"Good!" said her parents together.

"And there's always 'Food for Thought,'" added Mom.

"I know!" cried Molly. "'Windsor Volunteers Take a Bite out of Hunger!' How's that?"

"Perfect!" said Mom. "Then you can put the 'Serve up' pun in your article."

"Great, Molls!" said Dad. "The hardest part of writing your article may be over!"

As Molly headed back into the den, the phone rang. She sat back down in front of the computer and answered it.

"Hello?"

"Hello, I'm calling for Dish?" asked a woman. "My name is Bonnie Flynn."

"This is Molly Moore of Dish. How can I help you?"

"I saw you on *Good Day, America?* And I live in Park Terrace? I'd like to hire you to cook for me if you can."

"Please let me know when you'll need the food," Molly replied. "I'll talk to the other girls, and call you right back."

"Okay. I'll need dinner for three nights beginning next Tuesday. I have to go on a business trip, and my elderly mother and five-year-old son will be on their own."

"I'll call you tomorrow and let you know," promised Molly. She took Ms. Flynn's phone number, said good-bye, and hung up.

Molly smiled as she began to type in her fabulous headline. *This is fun!* she thought. *Now—let's see—I'll add a sub-head: 'To Serve Up Harvest Fundraiser in Prospect Park.'*

Yay!

As Molly typed, Amanda flipped through her science book upstairs, but her eyes weren't focusing on the page. Her mind kept going back to the audition. *I didn't do that bad, did I? Maybe I did...*

There's only one way to find out. I've got to talk to Ms. Barlow. Tomorrow.

Ugh.

The next afternoon in the cafeteria, the twins grabbed a table while Peichi and Natasha waited in line to buy lunch. As Shawn walked into the cafeteria, Amanda waved to get her attention.

Shawn nodded and headed in their direction.

Amanda flashed a grin. "It's nice to have Shawn eating with us all the time this year," she said. "At least *that's* going all right!"

"Yeah," agreed Molly. "And I think Shawn seems happier lately, don't you?"

Shawn had been the twins' best friend as long as they could remember. They'd met Shawn through Mom, who'd known Shawn's dad since high school. He and Mrs. Moore now both taught classes at Brooklyn College. When Mrs. Jordan died a few years ago of a long illness, the Moores did all they could to help Shawn get through it. She slept over a lot, and even spent weekends with the Moores on the New Jersey Shore in the big white house where Poppy, the twins' grandpa, lived. Shawn felt like a sister to the twins, but last year, when Shawn had met Angie Martinez through cheerleading, things had changed.

Shawn started hanging out a lot with Angie, and

eating lunch with the cheerleaders almost all the time. But the worst part was that Angie treated the Chef Girls terribly—especially Amanda. It seemed that she wanted Shawn all to herself. And when Elizabeth had joined cheerleading and turned out to be the best cheerleader on the squad because of her awesome gymnastic skills, Angie was so jealous that she destroyed Elizabeth's shoes just before a big cheerleading competition. When Coach Carson had found out, Angie had been suspended from cheerleading for the summer and fall.

Shawn had never known how to handle the complications that Angie created—which didn't help her relationships with the twins or Elizabeth. But Shawn had finally found the courage to make some big decisions when, during the summer, she'd realized the value of true friends.

"Wow!" said Shawn, placing her tray on the table. "I had the hardest math test this morning. It—"

"Hey, Shawn," called a shrill, familiar voice. "Hi, girl-friend! How *are* you? Come over here, I've been saving a seat for you!"

It was Angie, of course.

Amanda winced. *Uh-oh! I jinxed the lunch thing just by thinking about Angie.*

Shawn turned toward Angie and said, "No, thanks, I'm just going to sit here." She turned to sit down with the twins, her back to Angie.

Molly giggled. She was facing Angie and could see her

reaction. "Sara Schneider and Monica Timboli are trying to make Angie feel better," she reported to Shawn. "I think Angie's really annoyed you're not sitting there."

Shawn sighed. "I thought Angie had figured out by now that our friendship is over."

Natasha and Peichi joined Shawn and the twins with their lunches, and Molly brought up the charity harvest fair. "I'm definitely going to do it, and so is Elizabeth," she said. "Amanda, you will, too, right? So, what do you guys think? It would be *sooo* cool if you could help out. We'd have such a great time!"

"Sounds like fun," Natasha declared. "I'm in."

"I'd love to help!" agreed Peichi. "But I don't know if I can...you know, with the baby coming and everything..."

"But the baby isn't going to be born for six more months," Molly reminded her with a smile.

"Oh, right! Okay, sign me up! When are the meetings? What should we make? There are lots of awesome baked goods that are perfect for the fall! How about pumpkin pie? I love pumpkin pie! And apple cake and snickerdoodles and—"

"*Snickerdoodles?*" exclaimed the twins at the same time. "What are *those?*"

The Chef Girls burst out laughing—except Peichi, who looked surprised.

"They're awesome cinnamon sugar cookies!" she

replied. "You've never had snickerdoodles before? We'll have to make some! They're the best!"

"Let's make some for our next job!" Amanda said eagerly. The Chef Girls cracked up again. No one loved sweets as much as Amanda!

During last period, as Amanda sat in Ms. Barlow's French class, it was hard to concentrate on the vocabulary words she was supposed to be learning.

Maybe Ms. Barlow will have a few minutes after school today, Amanda thought. *So I could talk to her about why I didn't get a part in the play.* But just thinking about the conversation made her chest tighten.

The minutes dragged by until finally, the bell rang, and Ms. Barlow said to the class, "*Á demain!* See you tomorrow!"

Amanda waited until the class had cleared out. "Um, Ms. Barlow?" she began, her voice trembling. She took a deep breath and tried to steady her voice. "Can I talk to you about—something?"

Ms. Barlow's eyes widened. "Of course! *Certainment!*"

Amanda's toes curled tightly in her red leather shoes. "Um, I just wanted to know why—I didn't—you know...make the play." Her last few words were almost a whisper.

Ms. Barlow smiled sympathetically. "Ah, yes," she said with a sigh. "I've been meaning to talk to you, my dear, and I'm sorry I haven't yet. I know how you must feel! Why, a few years ago, I was *this close* to getting the lead in *Annie Get Your Gun*—for the national tour! I was really *'on'* that day for my callback audition. My voice had never been *better!* But you know, I didn't get the part." Her voice became softer. "And I was so disappointed—I've always wanted to play the part of Annie Oakley. Perhaps I never will." She lowered her eyes for a second, then shook her head quickly as if to get rid of the bad memory.

She smiled again at Amanda. "But this is *you* we're talking about." Her voice became more matter-of-fact. "My dear, there just wasn't the right role for you in this play. You know it's not a large cast this time, and—"

Amanda's heart began to pound so loudly she could hear it echoing in her ears.

"But I just got back from drama camp," she heard herself protesting. "I've gotten better! I'm a better actress now, a better performer!" Her eyes welled up with tears.

"Oh, darling, now *please* don't cry," clucked Ms. Barlow, magically producing a tissue. It smelled vaguely of her perfume. "I know you've improved—I watched your tape from Spotlight, which was *excellent,* by the way. But you know, even the most talented actresses—the ones we see in movies all the time—still need to audition for important roles. And they don't always get them! Sometimes

71

even the best actress just isn't right for a particular role."

"Really?" asked Amanda, confused.

"Here's a great example! You've seen *Gone With the Wind*, haven't you?"

Amanda nodded as she blew her nose.

"Well, can you picture anyone but Vivien Leigh as Scarlett O'Hara?"

Amanda shook her head. "No! Not at all," she replied.

"Can you imagine—Joan Crawford as Scarlett O'Hara?"

"Who?"

"Here, I have a picture of her in this book about the old Hollywood films...ah, here she is! A wonderful actress—but she would have been *terrible* as Scarlett! As famous as she was, she had to do a screen test—an audition on film. She wanted the part *desperately*. But she was awful! Just *ghastly!* And she wasn't the only one who was ghastly! The star Lana Turner was *just* as bad.

"You weren't ghastly, Amanda," Ms. Barlow quickly added. "But none of the roles suited you. That's all. And you know what? You *will* be in other plays. I *know* you will. And I do hope that you'll be involved in this play somehow, on crew. Please consider it. Okay?"

Amanda nodded numbly, then said robotically, "Thanks, Ms. Barlow. Uh, see you tomorrow." As she quickly headed out of the room, Ms. Barlow called, "Amanda? One more thing, my dear. If you're serious about acting, you must learn to deal with rejection. It's a part of the whole acting experience. See you tomorrow, and please cheer up! Everything's going to be fine."

Amanda smiled weakly, not even sure of what she was feeling. She knew she'd have to think over everything Ms. Barlow had said. *If you're serious about acting, you must learn to deal with rejection,* echoed her words.

I guess she's right about that, thought Amanda. *But can I deal with rejection? Do I even want to deal with rejection? It feels like my whole life is about rejection these days! I guess the big question is—do I like acting enough to face rejection again and again?*

"Yay!" cried Molly later that evening as she sat in front of the computer reading her e-mail. "Woo-hoo! I can't wait!"

Amanda rushed into the den. "What?"

Molly pointed to the computer screen. "See?"

To: mooretimes2
From: LiviaDeSanctis
Re: Hello from Aunt Livia!

Hi, Brooklyn Grrrlz,

    How are my favorite twin nieces? ☺

    I've been thinking about you a lot,

and Matthew, too! I spoke to your mom
today and told her that I'm coming
out to see you at Thanksgiving! It's
been too long since I came East. Your
mom promised she would let me tell
you...can't wait to see you! Hope school
is going well. We're going to cook up
a storm, aren't we?

Love,
Aunt Livia

"So that's why Mom kept smiling so mysteriously at dinner," grinned Amanda. "I'm so psyched!"

"Me, too!" cried Molly. "I haven't seen her in almost a year and a half! Hooray!"

Brrriiinnnggg!

"I'll get it!" called Amanda, running to the kitchen to get the phone.

"Of course you will," teased Mom from the living room.

"Hello?" said Amanda.

"Hello, this is Bonnie Flynn. I called a couple of days ago?"

"Er—yes? Who were you calling for?"

"I spoke to you about cooking three dinners for delivery next Tuesday. You were supposed to get back to me after you spoke to the other cooks?"

Amanda paused, confused. Then she realized what had probably happened. "Oh, you must have spoken to my twin, Molly!"

"That's right, I guess I did."

Amanda hesitated as she realized that Molly had never mentioned the call.

Uh-oh! I can't tell her Molly forgot to talk to us, thought Amanda. *But then, there's no other way around this.* She cleared her throat and said, "I'm so sorry, Ms. Flynn. I think Molly forgot to talk to us about this job...I'm sorry. I'll be happy to talk to the others myself and get back to you as soon as possible!"

"Never mind," said Ms. Flynn, who sounded impatient—and disappointed. "I really needed to know today. Thanks anyway."

Click!

Ms. Flynn had hung up.

Amanda winced. *Ouch. Well, I guess we deserved that.*

"Who was that, Amanda?" asked Mom, walking into the kitchen.

Amanda exhaled. "Well, it was a customer—I mean, an almost-customer. She called the other day and Molly forgot to tell all of us! So now the lady's mad and she doesn't want us to cook for her anymore."

"Follow-up is so important," said Mom. "People don't like to be kept waiting when they're trying to plan something. I'm surprised that Molly forgot! That's not like her at all—at least, not when it comes to Dish."

"I know," said Amanda with a heavy sigh. "What's up with that?" She walked back to the computer room, where Molly was busy writing back to Aunt Livia. "Um, Molls? Did you get a call from a Ms. Flynn a few days ago?"

"Oh!" cried Molly, slapping her forehead. "Oh, yeah! I can't believe I forgot to tell you guys! Uh-oh, did she call again?"

Amanda nodded. "And she said to just forget it, she really needed to know today."

Molly sighed. "Oh, no. I can't believe I did that. Well, I guess she'll never call Dish again. Rats! I feel so bad."

"Don't worry about it, Molls. Everyone forgets stuff sometimes."

But Molly still felt guilty about blowing off Ms. Flynn. *What's the matter with me?* she wondered. *I can't believe I forgot about a client! That's so bad for business.* Suddenly the IM bell rang on the computer, distracting Molly from her thoughts. An IM popped up on the screen.

To: mooretimes2; qtpie490; BrooklynNatasha
From: happyface
happyface: Hi, Chef Girlzzzzz! RUF2T? Do U want a job for a week from Saturday? For my neighbors across the street. And remember we have our other job for the Mortons this Thursday. LMK!

BrooklynNatasha: WFM

qtpie490: WFM 2!

mooretimes2: Hi, it's Molly. Manda can do it, but I can't make it B/C I said I'd baby-sit.

happyface: but Molly we need U! in case something goes wrong like last time! you saved the day remember? ☺ ☺

mooretimes2: just don't burn anything! Uh-oh, Amanda's not laughing ; -) TTUL.

"So, Amanda, what's up?" Molly asked her twin that night as they got into their pj's. "Are you feeling better about—the play?"

Mom poked her head into the girls' room. "May I come in?" she asked. She sat on Amanda's bed. "I couldn't help but overhear Molly's question."

Amanda nodded her head slowly. "Ms. Barlow made me feel a little better. I guess she's right—if you're gonna be an actress, you have to deal with rejection some-times!"

Molly nodded. "I guess it *is* a part of the whole acting thing."

"Have you given any more thought to costume crew?" Mom asked Amanda.

Amanda nodded. "Yeah. I think I will join the costume crew." She smiled at Molly and her mom. "I got some good experience working on costumes at camp. I mean, I'd still rather be *in* the play, but this is the next best thing."

Mrs. Moore put her arms around her daughters. "I think you're both doing great, and I'm so proud of you girls! You know, when I was in high school, all I wanted was to attend Steedman University and major in journalism—"

"But you went to Hawthorne College," interrupted Molly, puzzled.

"Well, that's because I didn't get accepted into Steedman," finished Mom.

"Really?"

"That's awful, Mom."

Mom nodded. "I was *so* upset. All my plans had been ruined!"

"So what did you do?" asked Amanda.

Mom shrugged. "I went to my number-two choice, which was Hawthorne. For my first semester, I signed up for an Art History class for my Fine Arts elective. Professor Palmer was wonderful! She got me so interested in all kinds of art from all times in history. And it didn't take long for me to decide to major in Art History. It turned out that Hawthorne was very famous for its Art History department, and it opened lots of doors for me! And now I have a job I love. So you see, sometimes things don't work out for a reason. I'm glad I didn't get into Steedman."

"Wow," said Amanda. "I guess this kind of thing happens to everyone, huh?"

Mom smiled. "I'm sure it does, sweetheart...you know, things that seem like failures often end up shaping us as much as our successes do. Remember, no matter what disappointments you face in life, tomorrow is a fresh start! Sweet dreams, my darling girls." Mrs. Moore kissed Molly, then Amanda good-night.

As Amanda snuggled beneath her puffy comforter, she felt comforted by Mom's words. *It's just one play*, she thought as she drifted to sleep. *Totally* not *the end of the world.*

8

The next afternoon, Amanda hung around after French class to talk to Ms. Barlow again.

"Ms. Barlow?" Amanda asked. "Um, I've been thinking— I'd really like to join the costume crew."

"Oh, I'm *so* pleased!" exclaimed Ms. Barlow. "You're showing a love for the theater that extends beyond acting—that you really want to be part of *every* aspect of the stage, even when you're not performing. The first meeting is next Monday, after school. Can you make it?"

Amanda nodded. "I'll be there, Ms. Barlow." As she walked away she thought proudly, *Ms. Barlow knows how much I love the theater! And now, I'll still get to be involved in the play.*

When Molly got home from school, she decided to start working on her Social Studies paper. She'd found a website on the internet for an organization called America's Second Harvest that had facts about hunger in America. *I can't believe what I'm reading,* Molly thought, shocked. *One in four people in a soup kitchen line is a*

child! Her eyes scanned the article further. *Approximately thirteen million American children were recently "food insecure," which means that they are hungry or at risk of going hungry...among families with children who visit America's Second Harvest, 76% are food insecure and 37% are experiencing hunger.*

Molly looked away from the screen. *How can that be?* she thought. *Food is so...basic!* She looked down at the apple she'd been munching on. She pictured the food that crammed the Moores' refrigerator and kitchen cupboards. *I've never gone hungry. Not even once. I just take food for granted. I never really stop to think that other people aren't as—lucky as I am.*

Molly sighed and looked back at the computer screen, at an article that said that hungry children were less likely to become productive grown-ups, because children who are hungry have more trouble learning in school—which can affect them for their entire lives.

This is so sad, she thought. *I wish I could help. But what can just one person do?*

That Thursday after school, the Chef Girls met up at the Moores' to cook a few dishes for the Mortons, who lived next door to Natasha. Mrs. Morton had just had a baby, and the Chef Girls were doing this job for free. It was the perfect night to do it, because there was no school the next day due to a teacher in-service day.

"Where's Molly?" asked Shawn.

"She must have had a *Post* meeting," replied Amanda. "But I can't remember. Anyway, I'll call Mom and ask her."

"Hey, guess what! I'm baby-sitting at the Minks' tomorrow night!" announced Peichi as she unloaded the grocery bags. "I can't wait. It'll be good practice for me!"

"Their little girl is so cute," said Natasha, who was washing her hands.

"And good!" declared Peichi. "Every time I see her, she's so quiet and happy! I hope our baby is like that," she added with a giggle.

"Well, I guess we should get started," said Amanda, glancing at the clock again. "I'm sure Molly will be home soon to help."

An hour and a half later, the Chef Girls had made a pasta salad, a bean-and-tomato casserole (something Shawn's dad loved to make), a lasagna, and were now onto the peanut butter cookie dough...and Molly still hadn't shown up. Amanda was annoyed.

"I can't believe Molly forgot about this job," said

Amanda, shaking her head. "That stinks! Oh, well, I guess Mom knows where she is." Amanda had called Mom's cell phone, but hadn't been able to reach her.

Just then, the front door slammed.

"Molly?" Amanda called out.

But it was just Matthew, who'd been playing across the street at the home of his best friend, Ben Bader. Matthew stomped into the kitchen. "What're you guys cooking?" he asked. "Peanut-butter cookies? *Awesome!* Can I have some when they're done?"

"Sure," Amanda replied. "But only a couple—these are for a client."

As they got back to work, the girls heard Mrs. Moore come home.

"Hi, Mom!" said Amanda.

"Hi, sweetie. Hi, girls. Hi, Matthew. Where's Molly? Upstairs?"

Amanda stopped. "Wait—you don't know where she is, either? Didn't you get my message on your phone?"

Mrs. Moore stopped looking through the mail. "I—I didn't check my messages," she admitted. "And I didn't think Molly had any plans today." She frowned. "What did she say the last time you saw her at school?"

"Not much. We had lunch together, but she didn't really talk about this afternoon."

"Well, that's strange." Mrs. Moore put her hands on

her hips and stared down at the floor, thinking. "Do you think she had at a meeting at school?"

The Chef Girls glanced at each other worriedly as Amanda shook her head. "I don't know. Meetings don't usually run this long."

Mom slung her big purse over her shoulder. "I'm going to drive up to the school." She left quickly.

"Do you think something happened to her?" asked Matthew anxiously. His hazel eyes had gotten big with worry.

"No, no," Amanda assured her brother. She smiled brightly and messed up Matthew's hair before he could duck away. "Molly's just so busy these days!"

But...what if something has happened to her? fretted Amanda to herself. *Molly, where are you?*

The kitchen grew silent as everyone waited for Mom to come back—and for Molly to show up.

Diiinnnngggg! went the timer, and everyone jumped.

"The cookies are ready!" cried Matthew. "Can I have a few?"

"Sure, just let them cool a minute," said Amanda absentmindedly. Her stomach was beginning to hurt. *Please let Molly be okay*, she thought.

Finally, the girls heard the creaky front door open, and Mom's and Molly's voices.

"Molly! Where were you?" cried Amanda, running into the front hallway, as the Chef Girls all sighed with relief.

"Sorry," muttered Molly. Mom, behind her, didn't look happy. "I was asked to cover the girls' soccer game against the Clinton Hill Cougars. I—I completely forgot about our job."

"And forgot to call to tell me where you'd be!" said Mrs. Moore angrily, heading upstairs.

Molly sighed and rolled her eyes.

"How'd you forget to tell both Mom and me?" asked Amanda, puzzled. "What's the matter with you?" Now that

85

there was nothing to worry about, she was beginning to feel annoyed with Molly again.

"I'm sorry," repeated Molly. She headed into the kitchen and said to the Chef Girls, "You guys, I feel so bad. I completely spaced out. I was so excited that Jayne Stein got sick and couldn't cover the game—I mean, I wasn't happy that Jayne's sick, but I was so excited that Liza asked me to sub for Jayne and then I was so nervous 'cause I've never written about a soccer game before! And I—just forgot! I'm really sorry."

Shawn, Peichi, and Natasha smiled at Molly while Matthew took the opportunity to scarf down some more cookies.

"It's okay, Molls," said Shawn. "There's still time to help us—we've got to box this stuff up and take it over to the Mortons'."

"Okay," said Molly. "Sure." She brightened as she said, "You guys! The game was great! Keisha White scored eleven points for Windsor! She's amazing!"

I don't even want to hear about it, thought Amanda, who was still irritated with her twin. *All of a sudden, Dish doesn't seem very important to Molly. And she doesn't even care that she worried Mom...and me! What's the deal?*

"Great, I'm grounded for the whole three-day weekend," complained Molly when she came upstairs after dinner, where Amanda was starting her math homework.

Amanda snorted. "I'm not surprised—Mom was worried! And, by the way, so was I."

"Oh, well, there's nothing I can do about it now," said Molly matter-of-factly. She opened up her notebook. "Manda, don't forget, we're having our first big meeting about the charity harvest fair on Monday."

"Don't worry, *I* won't forget." Amanda poked Molly in the arm. "I *never* forget!"

Molly didn't laugh at the joke. "It's really important that we do a good job on the fair," she said in a serious tone. "The money goes to America's Second Harvest. They're a great organization that helps feed people all over the country. Amanda, there are *lots* of hungry kids in this country. It's truly horrible. We *really* need to help. I want us to work really hard and raise as much money as we can. Okay?"

All right already, I get the point, thought Amanda, looking back down at her math book. *Why is Molly acting so different lately?* she wondered again. *Not calling and forgetting all about Dish was bad enough, but why is she talking to me in that preachy voice?*

After she finished her math homework, Amanda went downstairs for a cookie break. Mom was in the kitchen, reading a magazine. "Hi, sweetheart," she said. "I got you something from the library today." She reached into her leather briefcase and pulled out a very large book.

Amanda opened the heavy book. "What's this? 'The Costumes of Hollywood, 1930-1970.' Wow! This looks cool!"

"I thought it would inspire you—now that you're a costume designer!"

Amanda smiled at her mom. "I love it! Thanks!" She pointed at a woman in a photo. "Who's this?"

"That's Audrey Hepburn in the movie *Funny Face*. She worked with the French fashion designer Givenchy almost all the time—he created wonderful looks just for her."

Together, Amanda and Mom flipped through the big book, pointing at the gorgeous costumes. "This was made for Bette Davis by Edith Head," said Mom, pointing at an off-the-shoulder gown. "Edith Head was the most famous Hollywood costume designer."

"Look! Here are dresses from *Gone With the Wind*," exclaimed Amanda. "That's one kind of dress we'll be working on."

Later that evening, Amanda picked up a legal pad and began to sketch. She'd never been good at art, but it was fun to draw a gown that she imagined.

...And I think I'd put some lace here at the hem, she

thought to herself. *Maybe the same type of lace would go on the parasol, to match...*

Amanda smiled to herself. She couldn't wait to start working on the costumes with Ms. Barlow and the rest of the crew.

"You guys! *The Post* is out! With my article!" announced Molly the next afternoon as she set down her lunch tray. "And Natasha's, too, of course! There's a whole stack outside the newspaper office!"

"Let's see," said Amanda, as Peichi eagerly the paper. "Oh, look! 'Windsor Volunteers Take a Bite out of Hunger: Serve Up Harvest Fund-raiser in Prospect Park, By Molly Moore.' Cool!"

Natasha appeared at the table. "Oh, good, you got *The Post*," she said. "I heard it was out. Let's see your article...hey, there it is! And my interview with the new swim coach is on the next page."

"Cool!" said Shawn, placing her tray on the table. The girls passed the paper around as they ate.

"You won't believe this," groaned Peichi later, after Molly had set the paper aside. "You know how I decided to go out for Band? And—"

"Band? When did you decide to join Band?" interrupted Natasha.

"Yeah, I didn't know you were going to join the band," added Shawn.

"Neither did we," said Amanda, after seeing the surprised look on Molly's face.

"Oh! I guess I forgot to tell you!" Peichi giggled. "So much is going on! Well, anyway, I joined Band, right? And I was telling Omar and Connor about it. And the next thing I know, I'm in the band room, and Omar's in there, too! And he's like, 'Oh, hi, Peichi!' And he tells me that he's gonna play the *tuba!* Can you believe it?"

The Chef Girls shrieked with laughter.

"I can't picture Omar with a tuba!" cried Molly. "You mean he really plays the tuba?"

"No! He *doesn't* play the tuba!" said Peichi. "But he says he wants to *learn!* Like, all of a sudden, he's dying to learn the tuba after I say I'm in Band!"

"Why the tuba, I wonder?" asked Natasha. "Why not the flute, like you?"

"'Cause it was probably the only instrument Mr. Ciccone had left! Nobody *ever* wants to play the tuba."

The girls laughed again. The thought of skinny, wisecracking Omar playing the tuba just to be near Peichi was too funny.

"He must really like you, Peichi," said Natasha, giggling.

"But I don't *want* him there," groaned Peichi. "Every time I turn around, Omar will be right there—going 'oom-pa-pah' on that big tuba!"

The girls had a hard time eating their lunch after that—every time they calmed down, someone would say, "Oom-pa-pah" and they'd crack up all over again.

Later that day, Karen Woo's eyes grew wide as Molly and Elizabeth led Amanda, Peichi, Natasha, and Shawn into the cafeteria after school.

"Wow!" she exclaimed. "Are you all joining Windsor Volunteers?"

Shawn shook her head. "Not officially," she said, "but we're here to work on the harvest fair."

"We don't really have time to join another club," explained Peichi, "but we see this as, like, an extension of Dish, our cooking business!"

"We'll do tons of baking for the booth," added Natasha. "We're good cooks—and I'm sure we'll sell everything we make!"

"I know the theme for the fair is 'harvest,'" said Amanda, "but maybe we can make the theme for our booth a little more—broad? Wouldn't it be fun to have food from different cultures?"

Molly brightened. "Yeah! Our booth could be—what's

the word?—*diverse*, like Brooklyn! We could make some of the Greek food we had at Athena's!"

"And pumpkin ravioli," added Amanda. "That's harvest-y, and it's Italian!"

Just then, a few more students walked in.

"Hi, I'm Rachel," said a red-haired girl shyly. "Um, is this the volunteers' club?"

"This is it," replied Karen, flashing a smile at Molly that meant, *Thanks! Your article worked!*

"Okay, the main thing we need to focus on now is finding sponsors. They'll donate money so we can pay for the booth, ads, and supplies," Karen told them. "And the sponsors will have their names listed in the handout that tells all about the fair, and on the posters, too."

"I'll bet my dad would donate some money," Natasha spoke up. "He'd be getting free advertising for his new law firm."

Shawn turned to the twins. "Maybe Dad and your mom can get Brooklyn College to sponsor, too," she suggested.

"That would be great!" said Karen. "Let me know. Now, we need to find people who want to make crafts to sell."

Natasha looked up from the notes she was taking. "Um, my mom might do something. She's been painting a lot since we got back from France...mostly little paintings showing the streets of Paris, that sort of thing."

Karen nodded happily. "That would be good, because if

they're small, they wouldn't cost too much, and they'd make nice gifts."

Rachel's hand fluttered up. "How about pony rides?" she asked excitedly. "I have a pony! Her name is Misty! She's really sweet and gentle. I'll bet a lot of people would pay to let their kid ride her around, if you have room for her."

Everyone nodded enthusiastically. Their booth was going to be fantastic!

"Sure!" said Karen. "There's plenty of room—the fair is taking up a lot of land in the park that day!"

"What about other fun stuff?" asked Peichi. "For older kids?"

"How about renting a dunk tank?" Drew Hager, an eighth-grader, joked. "You know, where you throw the ball at the target and if you hit it, there's a guy who gets dunked?"

"That's a great idea!" agreed Peichi. "And I know just the guy to dunk!"

"Oh, really?" asked Karen.

Peichi smiled mischievously at her friends and announced, "Omar Kazdan!"

"I know him. Do you think he'd really do it?" asked Karen. All around her, the Chef Girls giggled. Omar getting dunked over and over in a tank of water? Way perfect!

"I'm sure he'll do it," Peichi assured Karen.

Then she added to herself: *If I ask him to!*

"Sorry, Dad, I need the computer again," Molly told Dad apologetically that evening. "I have to finish up the soccer game article *and* my Social Studies paper."

"I guess I can't put off buying that second computer any longer, can I?" Dad asked her with a grin. "Be my guest. I'm just surfing the Net anyway. But work on your paper first, all right? Then your article."

"I promise."

Childhood hunger is a big problem right here in the United States, Molly typed as she looked over her notes. *One group that helps with this problem is called America's Second Harvest. It runs lots of food banks. Thirty-nine percent of the people that get helped by America's Second Harvest are children who are under eighteen years old.*

Molly looked up from the screen. *How can this be? That's so many people!*

Suddenly Molly remembered that she needed to write a section for her paper explaining how she could help the situation. But what could she do? Molly frowned with determination. *I'll think of something. Even if I didn't have to do it for a grade, I'd want to think of something.*

"**S**o, Peichi, what happened?" asked Amanda eagerly at lunch the next day. "Did you ask Omar about the dunk tank? What did he say?"

Peichi giggled. "Yeah, I asked him in Band practice! He was like, 'Hi, Peichi, what's up?' and I was like, 'Oh, I'm fine, but I've got a lot on my mind,' and I told him all about the fair and said we really, really needed someone for the dunk tank and I was really worried we wouldn't find anyone! So he was like, 'Oh, I'll do it! That sounds like fun! And maybe I can get Connor and Justin, too!' and so I was like, 'Oh, really? That would be so cool!' as if I had never thought of asking him! So we've probably got three people for it!"

"Way to go, Peichi!" said the Chef Girls, giving her a high-five.

"Maybe we could get them to wear clown suits," suggested Molly. "By the way, how did your baby-sitting go the other night, Peichi?"

Peichi's face suddenly clouded over.

"It was a disaster!"

"What?"

"It was so hard! Little Joli was *not* happy. First of all,

she burst into tears the minute she saw her parents put their coats on. It's like she knew they were leaving, and she couldn't handle it! When they closed the front door, she started screaming *so loud* that guess what? She threw up all over the place! It was totally gross! And then I thought *I* was gonna throw up when I tried to clean it. So I made my mom come over to help! She said that kids Joli's age can have really bad separation anxiety when their parents leave. Mom calmed Joli down a little bit, but Joli just wouldn't stop crying! We tried singing to her and dancing with her, and reading to her, and playing puppets, and rocking her, but she just kept crying. Finally, she cried herself to sleep! By then my mom and I were so tired that *we* almost fell asleep while we waited for the Minks to come home." Peichi stopped to take a deep breath.

"I know what you mean," said Molly, thinking about her summer on Cape Cod with the Brewster kids. "Babies are a lot of work, aren't they?"

"Yeah," replied Peichi with a sigh. "And it just made me think about life in our house pretty soon. I mean, it's gonna be neat to have a baby around, but life will be totally different! My parents will be up all night with the baby, and they'll be tired, and the baby will cry a lot, and I'm gonna have to help out, and—and—"

"And you won't be the center of attention anymore," added Molly slyly.

"You guys! I didn't mean that!" protested Peichi, but when she saw the Chef Girls grinning at her, she had to laugh. "Well, okay, yeah—that, too."

"I hate to change the subject, but we have a lot to talk about," said Natasha, looking at her watch.

"Yeah!" said Molly. "First of all—Natasha, is your dad gonna be a sponsor of the fair?"

"Yes! He is!"

"Good. And Brooklyn College is sponsoring, thanks to Mom and Mr. Jordan. And everyone knows what we're going to bake for the fair..."

"That's easy," said Peichi. "And all we have to do now is help set up and run the booth. We've done all the 'do-ahead' stuff—except for the baking, of course!"

"And the decorations for the booth," Shawn reminded the girls. "I'm starting that pretty soon."

"But now we really have to talk about the haunted house," announced Amanda.

"Right! The haunted house!" exclaimed Shawn with a little laugh. "How could I forget? Man, we're gonna be *swamped* for the next few weeks."

"Oh, we'll get it done," Natasha assured her. "There are a lot of us."

"Yeah, and the fun food we're making isn't really that hard," Amanda pointed out. She pulled something out of her backpack. "I tore this out of Mom's magazine," she said. "See this salad? It's just peaches with faces cut into them to look like jack-o'-lanterns, with slivers of green apple for the 'stems,' and they're all covered in lemon gelatin!"

"Cu-u-u-te!" agreed the girls.

"I know how to make a skull out of a pear," Natasha told the girls. "You just carve it to give it a jawbone, scoop out holes for eyes, and put maraschino cherries in the eye sockets."

"And it's easy to make cute little ghosts out of bananas," added Shawn.

"How?" asked the girls.

"Oh, you just cut the banana lengthwise about halfway up, and put a craft stick in it, and carve out eyes and a mouth with a straw, and then you freeze it until it's time for the party."

"Gee, this food is so healthy for a birthday party," said Molly with a laugh.

"We'll make 'bat' birthday cakes," added Amanda. "They're so cute. You just buy one of those little frosted cake rolls for the body, and make an eight-inch chocolate layer cake for the wings. You freeze the layer cake, cut it in half lengthwise, and then cut curves into it to make it look like bat wings. Then you frost the wings with chocolate icing, and you use the icing to 'glue' on candies for the eyes and fangs."

"You use candy corn for the ears," added Molly. "So cute! We'll make a bunch of bat cakes."

All this silly stuff we're doing with food, she thought suddenly. *And meanwhile, so many kids in this country aren't getting enough to eat.*

And then she had an idea...

"You guys," she said abruptly, "after the fair and the Halloween party are over, I think we need to talk about Dish."

"What do you mean, Molls?" asked Amanda, as the Chef Girls looked at Molly curiously.

"Well, it's just that—that—maybe we should think about changing it a little," she said.

"Like how?" asked Peichi.

Wait a minute, I haven't thought this out yet, Molly wanted to say. But everyone was looking at her expectantly.

"Um, maybe we could do more charity cooking, like, doing more cooking for free for people who really need it. Wouldn't it be nice to just show up and give away hot meals?"

Four pairs of eyes stared at her.

"How would we make any money doing *that?*" asked Peichi matter-of-factly. The other girls giggled. Peichi always spoke her mind!

Molly rolled her eyes. "Well, it wouldn't *be* about making money."

Peichi shrugged. "But Molly, we have to make money with Dish. We can't spend money doing it—it's a *business.*"

She looked around at the other girls to see if they agreed with her.

Molly was turning red. "Well, some jobs would still be for money, and those jobs would pay for the food we give away..." She was thinking out loud now.

"Maybe we'd just be—what do you call it? Breaking even," said Natasha gently. "We wouldn't really be losing money, but we wouldn't be making any money, either."

Shawn nodded as Natasha spoke, and said, "You know, Molls, it's just that we're all so busy, doing our after-school activities and all our homework. I don't think that—that we really have time to put so much work into something that we were doing to make some extra spending money— which now wouldn't be making us any money."

"But—there are so many people out there who need help," said Molly.

"But we are helping!" Amanda reminded her. "With the harvest fair! We're gonna raise a lot of money for the hungry."

"That's true," said Molly. She shrugged. "Oh, well, I just thought it would be nice to do more 'giveaway' jobs."

"It would," said Amanda, as the other girls nodded in agreement. "But I think we have to find other ways to help besides cooking for free all the time. Anyway, we're doing a great job with this fair!"

Molly knew her sister and the others girls were right. So why did she still feel that she wasn't doing enough?

Later that night, Molly lay in bed, wide awake. She couldn't stop thinking of all the kids in America who were hungry right then—kids who couldn't sleep because their stomachs were empty, kids who couldn't sleep because they didn't know when they'd eat their next meal. *How can we make enough money for America's Second Harvest?* wondered Molly. *The fair is only one day. But it's a start. Wow, we're gonna need to bake a ton of stuff for it.* She worried that the Chef Girls' busy schedules—and getting ready for Matthew's party—would keep them from baking as much as they could. Her mind wandered as she thought about Dish...and the fun the girls had during the cooking class they took at Park Terrace Cookware...

That's it! thought Molly suddenly. *I'll get in touch with Carmen and Freddie. Maybe they can help!* Early the next morning before school, Molly typed:

To: pots-n-pans55; FredGonz528
From: mooretimes2
Re: help! (for a good cause) ☺

```
Hi, Carmen and Freddie,
How are you? Hey, Dish is baking up
```

a storm for a charity harvest fair at the Park in mid-October. Can you help us bake? Your fabulous pies and cookies and cakes would sell out! And maybe you'll become famous and start your own brand!? LMK, thanx a lot!

Molly Moore

"**H**ey, Amanda!"

Amanda turned around. There was Justin, standing right behind her in the cafeteria lunch line! "Oh, hi, Justin!"

"What's for lunch today?"

"Oh, the usual...Beefy Taco Casserole... mushy mixed vegetables...hey, it's Tuesday, you know!" Amanda wrinkled up her nose when she thought about the gross school lunches.

"So, Amanda, what's going on? Hey, Omar told me about the dunk tank!"

"Oh, are you gonna do it?"

"Sure! Omar and Connor and I all are. It'll be rockin'!"

"Great! Well, I'm—going to meet Molly and Natasha at that table over there."

"See ya. Oh, Amanda?"

"Uh-huh?"

"I'm—sorry that you didn't get in the play. But—you know, it sounds like a pretty lame play anyway. And you'll get in the next one—if you want to."

"Thanks, Justin. I'm, uh, working on crew, doing costumes."

"Hey! I just got a great idea! Maybe I'll do a photo essay and show the play from the very beginning until the night of performance! You know, show all the different people involved, and how it comes together. You better watch out...I'll be taking a picture of you in the costume shop!"

"Sounds good," Amanda said, smiling brightly at Justin. Then she had a great idea. "Um, Justin?" she asked, trying to sound casual. "Would—would you and Connor and Omar like to help out with something else? We're doing a haunted house for our little brother's Halloween birthday party, and we could use some creepy characters to hang out in it! It's the Saturday before Halloween, if you're interested."

"You mean, dress up like Dracula and stuff? Sure!"

"Great! I'll, um, e-mail you about it." Amanda grinned at Justin and walked over to the Chef Girls' table. She couldn't stop smiling. *He does like me...a little...I think!*

"So, I really think we should dress up as each other for Matthew's party," Amanda told Molly one morning as they walked to school. "Molly? Hello-o-o?"

"*Hmmm?*" asked Molly, who'd been deep in her own thoughts. "Uh, dress up as each other? What are you talking about?"

Amanda sighed. "*Molls!* Remember that idea you had for our Halloween costumes? That we'd dress up as each other? It'll be totally fun. We'll get you all dolled-up, and put glitter in your hair, and I'll wear your pine-green lowtop sneakers and your favorite beat-up jeans and your Brooklyn Dodgers baseball jersey. And, of course, I'll wear the ponytail! And then we'll see how well we fool people!"

"Oh yeah," remembered Molly. "That *was* a great idea I had! And when everyone ask us why we didn't wear costumes, we'll just tell them that we couldn't decide what to dress up as."

"I can't wait!"

"Me neither," said Molly absently. Her voice sounded far away because her mind was on something else—how she could help America's Second Harvest.

And how she was going to find the time to do it.

To: mooretimes2
From: FredGonz528
Re: Cooks to the rescue!

Hi Molly! Got your e-mail. I talked to Carmen and we both can help out. Tell you what—we'll donate 10 pies! OK? Just tell me where to drop the stuff off on what day. And you can charge a lot of $$ for them because they're made by the pie masters! ☺ ☺

    Freddie

    PS Carmen says hi!

"Today we need to start Becca's dress for Act II," Ms. Barlow told the costume crew one day after school. The crew of eight girls had gathered in the spacious storeroom that Ms. Barlow used to store all the props and costumes from past plays. Standing racks were crowded with dozens of costumes, cardboard boxes were overflowing with fabric and netting, and clear plastic tubs were crammed full of shoes. Hatboxes lined an upper shelf, strands of costume jewelry hung down from hooks, and an entire wall was covered with shelves holding props ranging from fake flowers to fake food.

Becca's dress.

For a split second, Amanda felt a twinge of sadness. Then she caught sight of the fringed red flapper dress that she'd worn in last spring's play, and she smiled. *I'll be on stage again,* she reminded herself. *Maybe sooner than later!*

She turned to Ms. Barlow. "Would you like a little purse to match Becca's dress?" she asked Ms. Barlow. "I can sew one up from the extra fabric. It won't take long. I could just make a tiny sack on a string."

"Perfect!" said Ms. Barlow, her sparkling brown eyes sending Amanda a grateful look. "Yes, she'll need one, since she'll be walking through town in this scene. *Wonderful* idea!"

Amanda picked up a pair of shears and began to cut a large circle out of the pink gingham fabric. The afternoon passed quickly with the girls laughing and chatting while they sewed and sketched with Ms. Barlow.

Amanda felt completely at home in the cozy, cluttered room. *This is the theater just as much as acting on stage is,* she realized. *It's just as important—and just as much fun!*

"I spoke to Athena," Molly announced to the Chef Girls when they'd arrived at the Moores' house the Saturday before the harvest fair for a baking marathon. "She saw my article in the paper and asked if she could donate some stuff to sell. I said, 'Absolutely!' So she's going to make spanakopita and that walnut cake we had at her party."

"Great!" said Shawn as she opened a new package of sugar. "And I talked to my neighbor, Mrs. Brooks. She's from Scotland. She said she'd make scones and donate them to the fair."

"Oh! I had a great idea! I'm going to

whip up some pesto sauce and bottle it!" added Molly. "I guess I'll go back to Choice Foods tomorrow for more basil and garlic and stuff."

"That's awesome!" exclaimed Amanda, who was stirring fresh cranberries into batter for cranberry-orange bread, a recipe from Mrs. Ross. "Can we talk about Matthew's party for a minute? You know, our other huge project? 'Cause as soon as we're done with the fair, we'll have to get to work on that."

The Chef Girls groaned.

"Hey, at least we have the three guys to help us. But we still have to decide who's doing what."

"Then we'd better call a meeting with Omar and Justin and Connor," suggested Natasha.

"OK, guys, settle down," said Peichi, sitting in a big booth between Justin and Omar the next day. The Chef Girls and Omar, Justin, and Connor had met up at Pizza Roma to talk about the haunted house. The boys were being rowdy—and people were turning to look at them.

Omar raised his hand. "Dude, I call Frankenstein," he said.

"You'll be perfect for that, since you're such a goon," Connor teased him. "I want to be Dracula."

"No, man, *I* want to be Dracula," protested Justin as he

reached for another slice of pepperoni pizza. "I have a tuxedo! I had to get it for a wedding once."

"Do you think your mom will let you wear it for this party?" asked Amanda. "You might get it all dirty."

"Sure," he said with a shrug. "I've almost outgrown it."

"Connor, I just figured out what you should do!" said Molly, snapping her fingers. "We'll make you look like a head on a platter!"

"*What?*" cried the group.

"It's so cool!" exclaimed Molly. "I saw it once in Park Terrace during the Halloween parade! Don't you remember, Manda? We'll get, like, a cheap card table at a thrift store, and have Dad cut a hole in it. And we'll stick your head through the hole! We'll cut a hole in a tablecloth and put it over the table so the kids can't see your body. And we'll decorate the table with food and napkins and stuff! And in the dim lighting, it'll look so creepy!"

Connor chuckled. "Yeah, let's make it look like just part of the party—it would be even better if we could cover my head with, like, a cake plate cover. Then the little kid comes over for some cake, takes off the cover, and I get to scare him to death!"

"*Ooohhhh!*" cried the friends, laughing.

"We'll try to do that," said Molly, "if we can find or make a cover big enough for your head—but don't forget, you have to be able to breathe."

"If we make a cover, then we can put air holes in," Natasha pointed out.

"Perfect," said Molly. She was sitting right across from Justin, and Amanda was next to her. *I was worried that this would be totally weird,* Molly though. *But everyone's cool!* She and Amanda were having so much fun that it didn't feel awkward for either of them to be hanging out with Justin.

"Oh!" exclaimed Omar. "I could make my costume so that one of my arms is inside my jacket—I'll borrow an old blazer of my dad's cause it'll be really big—and then we can make a papier-mâché arm. And we'll slide it up into the sleeve of my jacket. Then I'll shake hands with a kid, and when the kid grabs it, it'll fall off!"

"Do you really think that'll work?" asked Shawn, wrinkling her nose doubtfully. "Cause the arm won't go very far if it's still in the sleeve."

"Good point."

"Well, anyway," said Molly, "this party is gonna be great! Natasha, you're going to be a ghost, right?"

"Right!" replied Natasha eagerly. "I'll wear this old, long, white lace dress, and I'll put white powder all over my face and hands—"

"You should 'appear' in the living room once all the kids have arrived," interrupted Amanda. "And lead them downstairs into the haunted house!"

"Ooohh!" exclaimed Molly excitedly. "We'll make up a

story that you'll tell them—that this was your house, before something horrible happened to you!"

"That rocks!" said Connor. "Hey, is anyone gonna eat this last slice of pizza?"

Justin and Omar lunged for the slice just as Connor grabbed the crust. "Hands off! I called it!" Connor yelled.

"Dude, don't be a pig," Omar said, with his mouth full.

"Man, you ate, like, half a pizza yourself!" Justin said to Omar.

With a tug, Connor pulled the pizza toward him, and it split into three pieces. The boys scarfed down their last bite of pizza, then each wiped his hands and mouth on his shirt.

Amanda and Molly did the "twin thing" again. *So gross!* Then Molly smiled wickedly at her twin, leaned over and whispered, "They'll be *perfect* for the gross-out part of the haunted house!"

The following Saturday, the twins woke up early. It was the day of the fair!

"Oh, good," said Molly, stretching and looking out the large window. "It's going to be a sunny day—and probably warm!"

"That's good for the guys," laughed Amanda as she sat up in bed. "'Cause they're gonna get wet!"

"Think we should call everyone and make sure they're up?" Molly asked anxiously. "They have to be at the booth by nine!"

"Don't worry," Amanda reassured Molly. "They'll be there."

The Chef Girls and the Volunteers Club were pretty organized, but there was still a lot to do. Around eight AM, the twins and their parents arrived at the park, where Karen was already setting up the booth.

By ten o'clock, the bright sunshine had taken the autumn chill from the air. Prospect Park looked beautiful, with the red and orange leaves bursting on the trees. And the fair, set in the Long Meadow, looked amazing! Bright tents were everywhere. Clowns were putting on their makeup. Artists were displaying their crafts. Dozens of people hauled tables, wagons of baked goods, barrels, and bales of hay to various booths.

"Our booth looks awesome," said Molly proudly.

"It should," said Shawn as she began to tack up a sign listing the prices of all the items for sale. "We sure spent enough time on it!"

"Especially you," Molly told Shawn, grinning. "I love those felt autumn leaves you made for the awning. You're so artistic!"

"Look, there's Peichi with Mr. Cheng. They're bringing the apple cider. And there's Drew," announced Elizabeth.

"I hope Freddie will get here soon with the pies," fretted Natasha as she arranged her mom's little paintings on their tiny easels. "And that the boys aren't late."

Just then, a familiar voice called, "Hey there, ladies! The pie man has arrived!"

"And the pie woman," added a smiling woman with reddish-blond hair.

"It's Freddie! And Carmen! Hi!" chorused the girls.

Carmen waved with her free arm. She was carrying a basket of pies. Freddie smiled and made a funny face at the girls as he carried a box.

"Here are ten apple pies," said Carmen. "And we have ten pumpkin pies back at the car."

The girls helped arrange the pies in their booth.

"These are beautiful!" exclaimed Molly.

"Thank you, ladies. You humble me," said Freddie with a funny bow.

"Hey, I baked some, too," Carmen teased Freddie.

"I think we can get ten dollars each for these!" cried Amanda. "You're the best!"

"Check it out! It's Rachel and her pony!" cried Peichi. "*So* cute!" Everyone turned around to look at Rachel, who was riding Misty. The Chef Girls gathered around Misty and stroked her forehead. She was small and dappled and perfectly gentle.

"A whole bunch of little kids saw me riding her from the stable," said Rachel excitedly. "I told their parents what we were doing at our booth, and they're heading over as soon as the fair opens at eleven o'clock! Hey, look— they're delivering the dunk tank!"

The weather grew even more beautiful as the day went on, which brought more and more people into the park.

By eleven-thirty, the fair was jamming. Omar, Connor, and Justin had shown up right on time.

"Look, it's The Three Musketeers," joked Molly as they walked into the booth.

"Hi, Molly!" said Justin brightly. "I brought my camera. I thought I'd take some pictures for *The Post* when I'm not getting dunked!"

"Oh, that's a good idea," said Molly. "Um, maybe Natasha and I will write an article together."

"Sounds good," said Natasha, who was helping Shawn put up a sign advertising the dunk tank.

"Hi, Justin!" called Amanda from the other side of the booth.

Justin waved, but didn't come over to talk to her.

Rats, thought Amanda. *What's his deal?*

Amanda watched Justin closely, trying to read him to see if he liked her or not—or if he was still interested in Molly. But the truth was that, in front of his buddies, Justin pretty much ignored both of the twins.

As the boys helped set up the tank, a line soon formed with kids wanting to see the boys get dunked.

"Justin, you're going first, man," said Omar.

"No way, you are."

It didn't take long for someone to throw the ball right at the target, and down Omar splashed—making everyone laugh and yell.

"Man! That water's cold!" he cried, grabbing a towel.

When the little kids were bored with watching the boys make funny faces as they waited to be dunked, they went to Shawn's corner of the booth, where she was painting children's faces for a dollar.

"Oh, she looks so cute!" cooed Peichi, as a little four-year-old girl saw herself in Shawn's mirror and squealed happily.

Omar heard her. "Oh, she looks so-o-o cu-u-u-te!" he said in a high voice, imitating her, which made

Connor and Justin snicker. Peichi just rolled her eyes and called out to the crowd, "Get your fresh pies and holiday breads here! Freeze 'em for the holidays! They're going fast!"

Natasha's parents stopped by the booth to see if the girls needed help.

"Look, Mom!" cried Natasha. "I couldn't wait till you got here—see? Your paintings are selling! We've sold three Eiffel Towers and two Paris street scenes!"

Mrs. Ross gasped. "I—I can't believe it!" she said, amazed. "People are buying something I made!"

"Way to go, Mom!"

Mrs. Ross's voice softened as she looked tenderly at Natasha, saying, "Thanks, honey. But it was your idea." She quickly walked out of the booth, saying, "I have a few more at home—and I'm going to get them!"

The booth got busier and busier. For a while, the girls just saw a blur of new faces and green bills.

"Hey, the cranberry bread's all gone," announced Natasha happily. The Chef Girls had made eight loaves, and Mrs. Ross had made six.

"Good. So are almost all the pies!" exclaimed Amanda.

"The spanakopita is going fast," added Peichi, "and the walnut spice cake is long gone. We'll have to tell Athena how popular it was!" She giggled. "I bought some to take home tonight."

"Okay, my cookies are officially sold out," said

Elizabeth half an hour later, as she handed Karen the money from her last sale. "I can't wait to see how much money we made today!"

"I can't believe it!" cried Molly. She'd left her post taking money at the dunk tank to check on her bottled pesto. "My pesto sold out! I made twelve jars and they're all gone! Wow!"

"That's great, Molls!" said Amanda, then went back to helping Shawn.

This could really be something, Molly thought excitedly. *People want this stuff! I could sell it around Park Terrace at the little delis and gourmet shops, and give all the money to America's Second Harvest! Wow— this will be so cool! Oh—I want to do this more than any- thing. I've got to.*

She looked around the booth, practically bursting with her news. She was dying to tell her friends!

I can't bring this up right now, she thought. *We're just too busy. It's not the right time.*

But amid the chaos of the booth, Molly's heart slowly sank as reality set in. She wondered how she'd find the time to bottle her pesto sauce, sell it, keep up with her homework, cook for Dish, report for *The Post,* practice the piano, and be a better softball player next Spring.

Something's got to give, Molly realized. *But what?*

"That'll be eight dollars," she heard herself saying to a teenage girl. "Thank you! Two dollars is your change..."

What can I give up? I think I'm going to have to make a really big decision. The hardest decision I've ever had to make in my whole life.

By five-thirty, the sun was setting, and there was a chill in the air that reminded everyone that summer was over. People were drifting home, and the booth finally quieted down. Rachel left to take Misty back to the stable, the boys said good-bye, and only one of Mrs. Ross's paintings remained.

"Yay! We get to count the money now!" cried Peichi, as she watched Karen open the lockbox where everyone had been storing the money.

Fifteen minutes later, Karen looked up and announced proudly, "Five hundred and sixty-eight dollars for America's Second Harvest!"

"Woo-hoo!" cheered the girls.

"Wow! All our hard work really paid off!" cried Molly. She sat down, suddenly aware of how much her legs ached from standing all day. But she still felt great!

The next night, Peichi smiled into the lens of the digital video camera that she'd attached to a tripod.

"Hello, Baby Cheng!" she said. "This is your big sister Peichi! And this is the very first installment of the movie I'm making for you while we're all waiting for you to be born! It's a Sunday night, and"—Peichi began to giggle—"we had salmon for dinner, and now I'm going to interview our mommy...ready, Mom?"

"Ready," replied Mrs. Cheng, smoothing down her shiny black chin-length hair. She was seated on an upholstered bench in the living room.

"Now," said Peichi, beginning her interview as she looked through the viewfinder, "How many more months until the baby is born? How are you feeling? Do you want the baby to be a boy or a girl?"

Mrs. Cheng chuckled. "Your dad and I don't care if the baby is a boy *or* a girl. And I'm feeling fine! Just a little tired sometimes. Of course I'm getting a little bigger every week, it seems! The baby is due in just over five months. We can't wait until the baby gets here, but we still have a lot to do to get ready."

"Yes, like make up the nursery," said Peichi. "What color will it be, Mom?"

"Yellow," said Mrs. Cheng. "Definitely yellow."

Peichi looked into the lens again. "We still have to name you, Baby! It'll be a very special name chosen just for you! My name means 'precious jade' in Chinese!"

Peichi pointed the lens at her mom again. "And now, starting tonight, Mom and I are going to read something

119

beautiful before we go to sleep, because that's a Chinese custom, right, Mom?"

"That's right," said Mrs. Cheng. smiling. "According to Chinese tradition, what affects the mother's mind will also affect her heart and her connection with her unborn child. So, many Chinese women read beautiful stories before going to sleep."

"We're signing off for now," said Peichi to the camera. "Enjoy the story! Byeeee!"

Peichi turned off the camera. "So, Mom, what do you want to read?"

"Let's pick out a poem," suggested Mrs. Cheng, looking at the tall bookcase for a volume of poetry. "This is a nice tradition of our own, Peichi. I love it that we'll do this together every night."

Peichi snuggled up to her mom. "Me, too...Mom? Is it bad if I say that I'll kind of—miss, you know, just being together with you and Dad? Just the three of us, I mean..."

Mrs. Cheng stroked Peichi's hair. "No, it isn't," she said softly. "It *is* nice being the only child. But wait and see—I think you'll find that once the baby is here, it'll be such a part of us that you won't miss being 'just the three of us' so much."

"Okay," said Peichi, opening the book. "Anyway, we can make the most of it for the next five months, right, Mom? Now, which poem should we read?"

chapter 13

"**G**irls!" Mom called up the stairs. "Your friends are here."

"Oh! Good!" Molly called back. "We'll be right there!"

Justin, Omar, and Connor had arrived right on time to help get the haunted house together. It was two weeks after the fair, and Matthew's party was that night. While there was lots to do, the Moores had had plenty of help. The Chef Girls had been over all day helping Molly, Amanda, and Mom make the fun food. They'd left around three-thirty to go home and put on their costumes. Meanwhile, Matthew had been sent to the Baders' house to spend the day out of the way—and so that parts of the party would surprise him.

Amanda felt a little thrill of excitement knowing that Justin was right downstairs—but also because she couldn't wait to see how much fun Matthew and his friends would have at the party. "Well, I'm glad we figured out what we're gonna wear," she told Molly. "You'll look just like me in that dress I wore to the dance last year! Now, *sit still* while your nail polish dries. I'll curl your hair while we're waiting."

"Luckily for you, your costume is easy," teased Molly.

"For once, it won't take you *forever* to get ready for a party!"

Soon the twins were dressed as each other.

"Awesome!" they shrieked in front of the mirror.

"Oh, I can't wait to go to the dance," joked Molly, imitating Amanda.

Amanda struck a pose like she was at bat. "I'm gonna hit this one out of the park!" The twins cracked up. "Come on, let's get downstairs. Remember, from now on, you're Amanda, and I'm Molly."

"Okay, *Molly*," agreed Molly, with a grin.

Amanda and Molly hurried downstairs to the Moores' basement, which was looking even spookier than basements usually do.

"Wow, this is so cool, Mr. Moore!" Justin was saying as the twins walked in. Mr. Moore had just finished nailing a "coffin" together. "I can't wait to scare the kids with it!"

"Let's give it a test-drive," said Mr. Moore. "Hop in!"

Justin lay down in the coffin. Mr. Moore closed the lid and said, "You okay in there? I gave you lots of air holes."

"Great!" Justin replied, his voice muffled. The hinges creaked as Justin's hand emerged, pushing the lid open. He slowly rose out of the coffin, saying in his best Dracula voice, "Good e-e-e-ven-ing."

Everyone cracked up. Once Justin was in his costume and scary makeup, this was going to be perfect!

"So, when you hear Natasha leading the kids down-stairs, wait until you hear her say, 'Many spooky things live down here in the dark,' and then you can pop out!" Molly-as-Amanda directed Justin.

"Connor, let's get started on your 'table,'" said Dad. "We need to figure out how big the hole in the table should be for your head."

Just then, the doorbell starting ringing—and the twins shrieked excitedly each time they opened the door to find one of the Chef Girls in costume. Shawn looked great as the Bride of Frankenstein! Her costume was complete with a tall wig with gray streaks, fake bolts that looked like they'd been screwed into her neck, an old, yellowed bridal gown she'd bought at the Salvation Army, and high, clunky boots.

Peichi had two heads! Her mom had made a very realistic papier-mâché head that looked just like Peichi, complete with a long, black wig. She'd somehow managed to attach it to Peichi's shoulder, under her clothes. "I can't move too much, or it might get loose and fall off," Peichi told the twins and Shawn. "But isn't it cool? I'm so lucky my mom is an artist!"

Then Natasha arrived—and she really did look like a ghost! Her entire outfit was old-fashioned, from her black leather high-button shoes to her white lace dress with petticoats. Mrs. Ross had done an amazing job of making her up with white powder, even on her lips. And when she stared spookily at the girls, her cold, pale blue eyes looked incredibly creepy!

Elizabeth apologized for not looking scary, but she did make a very cute little Munchkin, with her red hair, striped tights, frilly short dress, and gigantic lollypop.

"Molly, why aren't you guys dressed up?" Shawn asked, looking at Amanda.

The twins couldn't help it. They started to snicker, then couldn't hold in their laughter.

"We are dressed up! As each other!" replied Molly from across the room, and the friends cracked up.

"That's *hysterical!*" shrieked Peichi.

"Wow, you guys haven't done that since you were, like, seven," laughed Shawn.

"Don't tell anyone," Amanda said. "The guys are downstairs getting ready. Let's keep it a secret from them."

The girls all headed down to the basement, where Mom was putting the finishing touches on the boys' spooky makeup.

"Wow, Mom! Great job!" cried Amanda. Connor's face was gray and sick-looking, and Mom had used black eye shadow to darken the area around his eyes. Justin's Dracula makeup was perfect, and Omar's face was a shade of grayish-green. The bolts in his neck matched Shawn's exactly. He wore a pair of his dad's old motorcycle boots, and they were so big on him that he walked just as slowly and clumsily as Frankenstein. "Mrs. Frankenstein, where's my dinner?" he asked Shawn, and everyone laughed.

During all the chaos of the last-minute preparations, Matthew came home to change into the cool robot costume that Mom had made. Amanda was arranging cookies on a platter when Justin walked over to her.

"Hey, Molly! This is gonna be a great party! But I can't believe you didn't get dressed up," Justin said to Amanda. Just then, Molly-as-Amanda caught her eye from across the room, and winked at her as if to say, *Poor Justin! He has no clue!*

Amanda pretended to cough so that she wouldn't start laughing really hard. "Well, we've been so busy planning this party, that, uh, we sort of forgot about our own costumes," she told him.

"Hey, did you catch the Yankees game the other night? Wasn't Yamamoto amazing? He's had such a great year."

"*Er*—yeah, amazing," replied Amanda. *Who's Yamamoto?*

"Who do you think's gonna go to the Super Bowl?" asked Justin.

"Um." Amanda shrugged as she desperately tried to remember the name of a football team—*any* team! "Well, I'm pretty sure it's going to be—uh—the Steelers."

"Against who?"

Amanda blushed, her mind working overtime. *What's the name of the New York team?* "Against, uh, the—Jets."

"Yeah! The Jets have a shot at it. Can you believe they traded Browning! Man! What a dumb move."

"Yeah! Can you believe it," said Amanda, shaking her head in fake disgust. Her acting skills were working overtime!

"And, you know, Emerson's out for the season," added Justin sadly.

What season? What team are we talking about? Are we still talking about football? wondered Amanda. "Yeah, he's—uh—not doing so great, is he?" Trying to change the subject, she added, "Guess what! Our parents are taking us to see *The Lion King* on Broadway."

"Cool," said Justin. "Hey, don't forget, the Tampa Bay-San Francisco game is on tomorrow. That's gonna rock!"

Wait a minute, Amanda suddenly thought as Justin droned on and on about football. *This is boring! I hate sports! I don't think Justin and I have that much in common, after all.*

Justin McElroy, I think my crush on you is finally over. Woo-hoo!

"This party rocks!" cried Connor an hour later. He was still hidden under his table, with his chin resting neatly on a piece of cardboard that Shawn had painted to look like a platter with garnishes of lettuce on it.

"Oh, Connor! You look so weird when you talk," Molly said, giggling.

"I really scared those kids," he bragged.

"Well, I don't know about that," commented Amanda. "They sure did laugh a lot when they pulled the cake-plate cover off your head."

"That's because they liked being scared," Connor insisted. "Help me out of this thing. I want some of that bat cake before the little rugrats eat it all!"

The twins cornered Matthew after he finished opening all of his presents. "So, Matthew, what do you think of your party?" they asked him.

Matthew grinned. "It's really cool!" he replied. "I liked it when Frankenstein came out from behind that curtain and scared everyone! *I* wasn't scared, though."

"Oh, no, of course not," said Molly, giving Amanda a wink over Matthew's head.

After the fundraiser and Matthew's party, Molly thought that life would quiet down a little—but she felt busier than ever. She had just gotten home from a *Post* meeting and was about to start her homework when the phone rang. As usual, Amanda grabbed it first.

"Hello? Yes, this is Dish," she said, grabbing a pen and a piece of paper.

Another Dish job? Molly thought, looking up from her notebook. She was trying to calculate the cost of ingredients for one batch of pesto sauce so she could figure out what to charge for it—and how much profit would go to America's Second Harvest. *Dish has been non-stop lately! I don't have time for this!*

"Three dinners next week?" Amanda was saying. "That shouldn't be a problem. I just need to check with my business partners. I'll get back to you tomorrow afternoon, okay?"

Molly sighed. *Great—Amanda practically just agreed to this job.*

"What's the matter, Molls?" Amanda asked as she hung up the phone.

"We've just had so many Dish jobs lately," Molly

complained. "I'm so busy! It's, like, hard to keep up. Maybe we should just skip this one."

Amanda frowned. "I don't know, Molly," she began. "It's an easy one. Besides, we really should check with everyone else to see if they want to do it."

"Good point," Molly admitted. "But I might have to bail. I'm sorry, Manda."

"No big," Amanda reassured her. "We did the last job with only four people and it went okay."

But it is a big deal, Molly thought as she looked at her list. *How am I ever gonna be able to do two businesses at once?*

"I'm going to e-mail everyone about the job," continued Amanda. "See you in a bit."

Downstairs in the den, Amanda turned on the computer and logged onto the Internet. Natasha, Shawn, and Peichi were all online, so she sent them an instant message.

mooretimes2: hey Chef Grrrlz! it's Manda. We just got a call from Mrs. Jacobson. She wants Dish 2 cook 3 dinners 4 Saturday delivery. Sounds easy. What do u say?

Qtpie490: I'm in! Thanksgiving is soon and u know what that means—CHRISTMAS is right around the corner! I have a ton of presents 2 buy and want to save up some $$$.

BrooklynNatasha: I'm busy Saturday but what about Friday afternoon?

Happyface: Fri. works 4 me!

Mooretimes2: me 2. I'll double-check with Mom to make sure we can use the kitchen. Oh yeah, forgot 2 tell u, Molls can't do this job. She sez she's 2 busy.

Happyface: Yeah, join the club!

Mooretimes2: Anyway, we can handle it! C-u 2morrow at school.

Amanda logged off the Internet and went back upstairs. "Everyone else is up for the job," she said as she walked into the twins' bedroom. "We're going to cook here on Friday afternoon, if Mom says it's okay."

Molly was sitting on the twins' windowseat, staring into space with an intense look of concentration on her face. She didn't answer.

"Hello? Earth to Molls?" Amanda joked. She was used to Molly's daydreaming. "What are you thinking about?"

Startled out of her thoughts, Molly looked up at Amanda. "What? Oh, nothing. That's, uh, great about the job. Sorry I can't help out, but I'm babysitting for the Brewsters on Friday." Molly hopped up from the windowseat. "I'm going to get a snack—you want anything?"

"Oh, yeah—would you bring me a cookie?" Amanda asked, her face brightening. "Thanks!"

"Be right back." Molly slipped out of the room and headed downstairs to the kitchen. *What am I gonna do about Dish?* she wondered. *I know one thing—I can't keep ditching our jobs. That's not fair to everybody else.* Molly sighed deeply. She already knew that there would be no easy answer to this problem.

A few days after the rest of the Chef Girls had done the Jacobson cooking job, Molly sat at the computer, her arms folded across her chest. She stared out beyond the screen for a while, thinking. After a few moments, she took a deep breath and began to type.

To: happyface; qtpie490; BrooklynNatasha
From: mooretimes2
Re: from Molly

Dear Chef Girls,
    I have an announcement to make. This is something I've been thinking about for a while. I'm sure you noticed that my mind hasn't really been on Dish like it was. It's been really hard for me to be involved in so many different things. And the

worst is that it's affected you guys, and our business, like when I forgot that client called, and forgot to show up for a job. My crazy busy life shouldn't hurt our business.

That's why I've decided to leave Dish. This is something I've been thinking about non-stop for a couple weeks now. I really want to do some new things, like seeing if I can make my own pesto sauce and sell it around Park Terrace for charity. Maybe that's just a dream—but I really, really want to help people. And I want to keep trying new activities at school, too.

I hope you won't be mad at me, but if you are, you are. I guess there isn't anything I can do about that. I know you guys can handle Dish—you're awesome! I'll miss Dish, but I still love you guys. We'll always be BFFL.

Lots of Love,
Molly

Molly sighed, hit "SEND," then stood up and got ready to go tell Amanda her news.

happyface: whoa! Did u see Molly's EM!?!?!?
BrooklynNatasha: i'm in shock!
qtpie490: wow. I can't believe she didn't call 2 tell me. But I think this was the easiest way for her to deal with it. anyway, I'm really surprised!! I wonder what Amanda is feeling right now!
BrooklynNatasha: Well, I guess Molly did it 4 dish, since she's kinda, well, not been there, and we did that last job w/out her anyway B/C she was baby-sitting.
happyface: no—the last 2 jobs!
BrooklynNatasha: whoops, oh yeah!
qtpie490: L8R chef grrrlzz. GTG, but anyway we won't give her a hard time 2morrow.
happyface: so sad! But oh well. C U 2morrow.

"Hi. What are you doing?" Molly asked Amanda up in their room. She could barely breathe, knowing that she was about to tell her sister the bad news. Between the summer-with-Justin news, and now this, she'd been doing that a lot lately.

133

"Oh, I'm just sketching a costume idea I had," said Amanda as she retraced a few lines on her paper. She looked up. "Molls, what's up? You look so worried."

Her heart pounding, Molly replied, "I'm, uh, not going to be cooking. With Dish."

"Huh?" Amanda frowned, trying to figure out what Molly meant. "We don't have a Dish job this week, Molls. The one you couldn't make was *last* week."

"No. I'm—leaving Dish, Manda."

"*What!* You're quitting *Dish?*"

Molly nodded, not taking her eyes off Amanda's face.

"B-but—you're, like, the leader of Dish! *Why?*"

"Well, I—I'm just too busy these days, Manda. And I want to do a new business. I want to bottle pesto sauce and sell it around Park Terrace. Then I can donate all the proceeds to charity."

"Are you *kidding?*" Amanda exclaimed. "Molly, I know the whole charity thing is important to you, but Dish is our—our *business!* You don't just *quit* a business on a whim, Molly! You can't dump the whole thing on my head! It's not *fair!*"

"You know what's not fair?" Molly snapped. "The fact that so many kids in this country go hungry—*every single day*. And I want to—want to help them. It has nothing to do with *you.*"

"Of *course* it does!" Amanda replied, her face growing hot. "Who's going to take over Dish? Everyone else is busy, too. I can't *even* believe you would just *quit* like that, like it's no big deal! You know what? Forget it. This is too much. *Everything* has been going wrong lately. I can't take one more thing!"

"Oh, *please*," Molly rolled her eyes. "Your life is great. We are so incredibly—*blessed* and we don't even know it!"

"Oh, all *right* already, little Miss—Miss—" sputtered Amanda, annoyed that she couldn't come up with the right put-down. "...Save-the-World!"

"Little Miss Save-the-World" sounded so corny as it came out of her mouth that Amanda had to snicker at herself. She quickly tried to turn it into a sound of disgust at her sister, but Molly was too quick. She heard the laughter trying to come out, and suddenly, Molly was laughing, too.

Molly took a deep breath. "Listen, Manda," she began seriously. "This was, like, the hardest decision I've ever had to make. And you're right—this does affect you. And I'm sorry if you're upset with me. I hope—I hope you can understand that this is just something I have to do right now."

Amanda nodded. She understood, suddenly, what her sister was saying. "Well, you have to do what you have to do, I guess. Dish won't be the same without you, though."

Molly smiled thankfully at her sister. "Thanks, Manda. But I'm not going anywhere. Maybe I can still help out sometimes. We'll just...see how it goes."

She reached out her arm to help Amanda up. "And we'll still cook together. I don't know about you, but I could totally go for some brownies. How 'bout it?"

Amanda smiled at Molly. "Sure thing. Let's go make some." As Amanda followed her twin downstairs, she realized, *It's gonna take a while to get used to Molly not being in Dish. But I got used to Justin liking Molly instead of me. And I got used to not being in the play. These things just take...time.*

chapter 15

"**O**nly a few more hours!" cried Molly when she met up with Amanda in the cafeteria the next afternoon.

"Yeah," said Amanda. "I can't wait to get home!"

"What's going on?" asked Peichi as she sat down with the twins at their favorite table.

"Aunt Livia flew in this morning," replied Molly, looking up at the big clock that hung over the cafeteria door.

"Oh, yeah!" said Peichi, brightening. "Can I meet her? She sounds cool! Boy, am I ready for our vacation break. That math test was so hard today. My brain hurts! I just want to lie around and eat turkey and—"

"Watch movies," said Shawn, digging into her chili.

"Sleep in!" giggled Elizabeth.

"Read whatever I feel like, instead of text- books," added Natasha.

"Cook!" said the twins at the same time.

"Aunt Livia is a really good cook," Amanda told the friends as she picked at her green beans. "As good as Mom. And she's gonna make lots of stuff with us.

"She was joking that Mom always makes her cook when she comes to visit," said Molly, "but she loves to just get in the kitchen and take over. Our Thanksgiving dinner is gonna be awesome!"

"You guys, I can't believe it's Thanksgiving already," said Shawn. "So much has happened since school started!"

Everyone nodded.

"Yeah," chuckled Peichi. "Lots of changes! I wonder what's gonna happen next!

No one said anything for a moment.

"I was wondering when you were going to bring up my e-mail," said Molly, looking at Peichi.

Peichi turned to Molly. "We're really gonna miss you, Molly. I don't want to make you feel bad, but...gee, it's gonna be totally different."

"You guys will do just fine without me," Molly said with a smile. She turned to Elizabeth. "Elizabeth, are you sure you don't want to join Dish and take my place?"

"I'll think about it," replied Elizabeth. "I like cooking and all—but I'm not sure I like it *that* much."

The table got quiet again.

"No one else is gonna quit, right?" asked Amanda anxiously.

Everyone shook their heads.

"Oh, good. I don't think I could take any more big changes right now!"

"Yay! You're here! You're really here!" cried the twins that afternoon. They ran into the kitchen and threw themselves at Aunt Livia for major hugs. She smelled of the lavender soap she'd been using since she was a teenager. Her hair had been clipped stylishly short, and her small sapphire earrings gleamed.

Aunt Livia held Molly back at arms' length. Her dark eyes grew wide in surprise.

"I'm here! Wow! Look at you! You're both so big! And gorgeous!"

"Big and gorgeous, it runs in the family," joked Mom.

"We have you, and school's out for the break! How lucky can we get!" exclaimed Molly.

"Molly, you've changed!" said Aunt Livia. "I mean, I've seen Amanda recently, but you—you seem different!"

"Oh, boy, is she different all right," said Amanda, rolling her eyes. "She's changing by the hour. I'm just trying to keep up!"

"You seem different, too," Molly teased Aunt Livia, running her hand over her hair. "I see some gray hairs in your new short haircut!"

"I noticed that too, Livie," Mom said with a laugh. She poked her sister playfully. "I didn't think people got gray hairs living in California!"

"Doesn't matter. Now I've got all my girls around me," said Aunt Livia. "Tell me, tell me everything, and if you're good, maybe I'll show you a picture of my *boyfriend.*"

"Boyfriend!" squealed everyone, even Mom. "Let us see it right now!"

The next morning, Molly and Amanda felt a light touch on their backs.

"Girls," whispered a soft voice. "Do you want to help me with the turkey? I've made you some hot chocolate."

"Sure, Aunt Livia," murmured Molly drowsily. "Come on, Manda, get up. It's Thanksgiving morning!"

"What are we gonna make?" Amanda asked her aunt sleepily. "Besides turkey, I mean?"

"Come downstairs and find out, sweetheart. The turkey and I are having coffee."

"Huh?" muttered Molly, too sleepy to get the joke.

The twins washed their faces, changed into cozy sweats, and quietly headed downstairs. It was so nice to see Aunt Livia there, knowing they'd have her all to themselves for a little while.

"Oh! The Macy's Thanksgiving Day Parade is about to start," said Molly. She turned on the tiny TV that Mom kept on the counter.

Aunt Livia brightened. "Right! You know, your mom and I went to that a few times with our friends when we were teenagers. But the best part was the night before the parade—you used to be able to watch the balloons getting inflated!"

"So what's on the menu?" Amanda asked.

"We'll have oyster stew to start with," Aunt Livia told the girls. "We'll make that later. You'll love it."

"I'll bet Matthew won't," giggled Molly.

"Sure he will! And we'll make a nice fig and sausage stuffing for the turkey. Your mom and I bought everything we need."

"That's different," stated Molly. "Mom usually makes stuffing without meat."

"Can we have broccoli with cheese sauce tonight? Please?" asked Amanda.

"Sure! Okay, let's get started on the piecrust," said Aunt Livia. "I had a terrific apple-cranberry pie in a restaurant recently, and I'm dying to make one!"

"We already made the piecrust, Aunt Livia," Molly said proudly. "I'll get it out of the freezer!"

"*Mmm*. I can't wait to taste your piecrust."

"I'll make the cranberry sauce," offered Amanda. "That's easy. And then we can chill it in the fridge all day."

"Now," said Aunt Livia, "Molly, let's start frying this sweet Italian sausage for the stuffing. I'll chop the onion, okay?"

"Oh, good," said Molly, relieved. "It's just too early for me to think about chopping an onion!"

"*Mmmm*," said Amanda contentedly as she began to

cook the cranberries. "Thanksgiving is the most delicious holiday!"

Hours later, the big house was full of great smells: the roasting turkey, which the twins took turns basting every twenty minutes...the fresh-baked apple-cranberry pie that cooled on the counter...Mom's homemade dinner rolls, keeping warm by the stove.

In the family room, the TV was on all day. The parade was over, and now it was time for football! Dad and Matthew wandered back and forth between the kitchen and the family room, helping and watching the big game at the same time—though Matthew did more snacking than helping.

The twins took their time setting the table after Mom covered it with her best lace tablecloth, the one that Nana had brought from Italy. They made it sparkle with china dishes, crystal goblets, and gleaming silverware.

Everyone dressed up a bit—even Matthew. Amazingly, he'd put a clip-on tie on his good shirt—without any special request from Mom!

"It's Livia," whispered Mom to the twins. "He did that for her!"

Aunt Livia was still in her jeans, humming and making the oyster stew.

The twins and Mom stayed in the kitchen with her as she drained the oysters and added them to the chopped celery and onion that was cooking fragrantly on the stove. "I'll cook these oysters slowly until the edges curl slightly," she said. "...Now we add the boiling milk and heavy cream...the Worcestershire sauce...and now the Tabasco sauce! Okay! I'm going to put on a dress and some lipstick. Now heat that until the oysters are fully curled, girls. Add a little salt, and then it's time to garnish it with Molly's chopped chives—and eat it!"

The family sat down at the high-backed chairs in the dining room. The turkey was carved and Mom had dimmed the lights of the chandelier. Another Thanksgiving dinner was about to begin.

Everyone looked expectantly at Dad—it was time for him to say grace. All bowed their heads as Dad gave thanks for family from far away, the wonderful food, this special day...

And then it was time for the clinking of glasses, and "Pass the mashed potatoes, please," and watching Mom and Aunt Livia laugh girlishly together.

Molly paused as she watched the happy scene before her. The faces of her family glowed in the candlelight as they shared dish after dish with each other. *I have so much to be thankful for,* she thought. *I wish every kid had what I had!*

And then she got goose bumps...because something was dawning on her. An idea. No—a decision. It was something big and exciting and a little bit scary because it seemed so...real.

That's it! I'm going to make helping kids my career when I grow up. I can't wait!

"Molls? Do you want some gravy?" Amanda asked softly, as if she knew she was interrupting her sister's thoughts. "Here."

Molly took the gravy boat and smiled at her twin.

I may change a lot, and so will Manda. But we'll always be close, just like Mom and Aunt Livia. And no matter what, we'll make big, yummy Thanksgiving dinners together, every year with our families. 'Cause some things should never change!

The Amazing cookbook

By

The CHEF Girls

AMANDA!
Molly!
Peichi ☺
shawn!
Natasha!

Freddie's
Fabulous Pumpkin Pie Filling

My pumpkin pie is the best, and I'll tell you why!
I add grated orange rind. It adds a nice tang
to it! Trust me—you'll love it!

You will need to make or buy
a 9-inch, one-crust pie shell.

Preheat oven to 425 degrees.

Beat all of these ingredients together with a mixer:

1¾ cups mashed cooked pumpkin

½ teaspoon salt   ¼ teaspoon cloves
1¾ cups milk   ½ teaspoon ginger
3 eggs   ½ teaspoon nutmeg
⅔ cup brown sugar   grated rind from 1 orange
2 tablespoons sugar
1¼ teaspoons cinnamon

1. Pour this mixture into a
   pastry-lined 9-inch pie pan.

2. Bake for about 45 minutes. The center may still
   be a bit soft, but don't worry, it'll set later.

3. When you're ready to serve this, top with whipped cream. Do me a favor? Don't use the stuff in the plastic tub or the can! Your pie is too good for that! This is the way to make real whipped cream, and it's so easy! Now you're high class!

Whipped Cream

½ pint whipping cream
½ teaspoon vanilla extract
½ teaspoon orange flavoring (optional)
¼ cup sugar

NOTE: Whipping cream whips faster if it's cold. Have your mixer blades and bowl chilled before you start.

Pour chilled whipping cream into a mixer bowl, and beat on "High" until it starts to thicken. Gradually add the sugar. Add the vanilla and orange flavorings and continue to whip until thick enough to hold peaks. Now, wasn't that easy? Keep it chilled until ready to serve.

Karithopita (Greek Walnut Cake)

I love to make this with my mom!

FOR THE BATTER

Flour Mixture:

2 cups flour
1 teaspoon baking powder
1 teaspoon baking soda
1/2 teaspoon nutmeg
1/2 teaspoon cinnamon
1/2 teaspoon ground cloves
1 cup coarsely chopped walnuts

Wet Mixture:

2 cups sugar
2 sticks butter, softened
6 eggs
1 cup sour cream

Preheat oven to 325 degrees. Grease and flour 13" x 9" x 2" glass baking dish and set aside.

1. Combine flour mixture ingredients in a large bowl and set aside.

2. Make the wet mixture in another large bowl. Beat the sugar and butter until creamy. Beat in eggs, adding one at a time. Beat in sour cream until well blended.

3. Slowly add flour mixture to wet mixture. Stir in walnuts by hand.

4. Add batter to prepared baking dish. Bake for 35 - 40 minutes, or until top springs back when lightly pressed

and a wooden toothpick inserted in center comes
out clean. Remove from oven and allow to cool
completely before adding syrup.

FOR THE SYRUP:

1 ½ cups sugar   Peel of orange or lemon
1 cup water   2 OR 3 2-inch cinnamon sticks
Optional garnish: Maraschino cherries

1. In a medium-sized saucepan, combine sugar, water,
   orange or lemon peel, and cinnamon sticks.
2. Bring to a boil, stirring constantly until sugar is
   dissolved. Boil slowly for 10 minutes. Remove from
   heat and allow to cool.
3. Remove peel and cinnamon stick and pour syrup
   over cooled cake. Allow cake to rest until syrup
   is completely absorbed.
4. Cut cake into diamonds or squares and
   place in aluminum baking cups. Garnish
   with Maraschino cherries.

The cake can be frozen, if you cool it completely,
cut into pieces, and tightly wrap it.   —Athena

"Emergency" Biscuit-topped Chicken Potpie

PLACE IN LARGE BOWL:
3 to 4 cups cooked chicken, cut into bite-size pieces. (Get ride of the skin and bones if you're taking from a roasted chicken.)

THEN ADD AND MIX TOGETHER:
1 can cream of chicken soup
1 can cream of celery soup

1 1/2 cups milk
1/2 teaspoon salt
1/4 teaspoon pepper
dash of poultry seasoning
1 package of frozen corn in butter sauce
1 package of frozen peas in butter sauce
1/4 cup sliced baby carrots (slightly cooked)

Pour this mixture into a 9" x 12" baking dish.

Molly saved the day with this one! I made it for my dad later and he really liked it! this recipe makes a lot—we had 3 meals out of this, and that was with having more than one helping.

—Shawn

ADD:

1 package large refrigerated biscuits (8 count) cut in half.

Place evenly on top of chicken mixture. Sprinkle with parsley, celery seeds, and paprika. Bake at 450 degrees for 35 minutes, or until biscuits are browned on top.

cooking tips from the chef Girls!

The Chef Girls are looking out for you!
Here are some things you should
know if you want to cook.
(Remember to ask your parents
if you can use knives and the stove!)

1 Tie back long hair so that it won't
   get into the food or in the way as
   you work.

2 Don't wear loose-fitting clothing
   that could drag in the food or
   on the stove burners.

3 Never cook in bare feet or open-toed
   shoes. Something sharp or hot could
   drop on your feet.

4 Always wash your hands before you
   handle food.

5   Read through the recipe before you start. Gather
    your ingredients together and measure them
    before you begin.

6   Turn pot handles in so
    that they won't get
    knocked off the stove.

7   Use wooden spoons to stir hot liquids.
    Metal spoons can become very hot.

8   When cutting or peeling food,
    cut away from your hands.

9   Cut food on a cutting board,
    not the countertop.

   10   Hand someone a knife with the
                            knifepoint pointing to the floor.

                       11   Clean up as you go. It's safer and neater.

12 Always use a dry pot holder to
    remove something hot from the
    oven. You could get burned with a
    wet one, since wet ones retain heat.

13 Make sure that any spills on the floor are cleaned
    up right away, so that you don't slip and fall.

14 Don't put knives in clean-up water. You could reach into the water and cut yourself.

15 Use a wire rack to cool hot baking dishes to avoid scorch marks on the countertop.

An Important Message from the Chef Girls!

Some foods can carry bacteria, such as salmonella, that can make you sick. To avoid salmonella, always cook poultry, ground beef, and eggs thoroughly before eating. Don't eat or drink foods containing raw eggs. And wash hands, kitchen work surfaces, and utensils with soap and water immediately after they have been in contact with raw meat or poultry.

Instant messaging and e-mail dictionary!

dish

mooretimes2: Molly and Amanda

qtpie490: Shawn

happyface: Peichi

BrooklynNatasha: Natasha

JustMac: Justin

Wuzzup: What's up?

Mwa smooching sound

G2G: Got To Go

deets: details

b-b: Bye-Bye

brb: be right back

<3 hearts

L8R: Later, as in "See ya later!"

LOL: Laughing Out Loud

GMTA: Great Minds Think Alike

j/k: Just kidding

B/C: because

W8: Wait

W8 4 me @: Wait for me at

thanx: thanks

BK: Big kiss

MAY: Mad about you

RUF2T?: Are you free to talk?

TTUL: Type to you later

E-ya: will e-mail you

LMK: Let me know

GR8: Great

WFM: Works for me

2: to, too, two

C: see

u: you

2morrow: tomorrow

VH: virtual hug

BFFL: Best Friends For Life

:-@   shock

:-P   sticking out tongue

%-)   confused

:-o   surprised

;-)   winking or teasing